About the Author

Hazel Williams began her nursing career in 1948 and has worked in the NHS for many years. In hospitals, as a School nurse, Queens District nursing sister and nursing management. She is married to Neville, they have two children, one son and daughter, three granddaughters and one grandson. They have enjoyed travelling around the world, although most of her life has been in Nottinghamshire, where she has enjoyed being active in Christian work with all ages of people.

Best Wishes
Hazel Williams

Dedication

This book is dedicated to my husband, Neville and daughter Rachel for their help with this computer!

Hazel Williams

THE ALPHA HOME

AUSTIN MACAULEY
PUBLISHERS LTD.

A CIP catalogue record for this title is available from the British Library.

ISBN 978 1 78455 669 3

www.austinmacauley.com

First Published (2015)
Austin Macauley Publishers Ltd.
25 Canada Square
Canary Wharf
London
E14 5LB

Printed and bound in Great Britain.

Chapter 1

Bethany's parents were enjoying their holiday of a lifetime, a cruise around the Spanish and Greek Islands. Today they were going ashore to visit Quadalest, a monastery high in the mountains; the mini bus picked them up at the ship, along with eight others, to begin the journey up winding roads, beautiful scenery and the promise of a good lunch at the end of the journey. The lovely scent of the flowers and trees wafted in through the open bus windows although they became rather uneasy as the driver took the frequent bends rather too fast. Suddenly there was a lurch and the driver lost control of the wheel, there were screams as the minibus plunged onto the tree tops in the valley below. The silence could only mean the people were unconscious or had lost their lives.

Beth was getting ready for bed, one last look outside at the animals near to the farm, also to lock the hens safely; the fox liked to get into them. This was a lovely old farm, the house always warm and friendly. Everyone was welcome here, her mother made sure they had a cup of tea and farmhouse cake before they left. The night air was warm and balmy and Beth knew it was no problem to keep house whilst her hard working parents went on a well-deserved holiday. The couple who worked on the farm lived in a cottage next to the house Beth called them auntie and uncle as they had known her since she born! Sitting on the seat under the apple tree she thought of her work in London. How she had wanted to be a nurse. She enjoyed caring for people also working in her spare time with Father Joseph in St. George's crypt giving soup and comfort to those living on the streets in London. Sometimes she had helped different ones to get back to their family, also telling them of the love God has for them and a different way of life they could have if they trusted in Him. Beth was an only child she felt sad that there was no son to take over the farm when Dad retired. However her faith was strong. She had committed her life to Christ, so He had a plan for her, she was sure. Little did she think her faith would be "tried" in the very near future. Thinking of her parents, basking on the deck of the cruise ship, she made her way to bed.

The shrill sound of the telephone woke Beth the next morning. Slipping out of bed she could not imagine who would be ringing at 6 a.m. The local police officer asked her to come down to the station and bring someone with her.

"What is it all about?" she asked. "Has someone been stealing our cattle?

"No, nothing like that. See you within the hour." With that he rang off.

She quickly got dressed and called Kate Jackson, the farm manager's wife, who came immediately. Bill was busy with the cattle, so they went alone. At the police station they were given tea and biscuits and seated in the chief's office.

"I have known you, Beth, for a long time, and what I have to tell you is most distressing. Your parents have been in an accident in Spain whilst visiting a monastery. Their minibus left the road and went down a ravine." Beth gasped. "They were on a cruise not on mainland Spain," she said. "There must be some mistake."

"They are pretty sure they are right and I am devastated to have to break this news to you. The authorities would like you to go to Spain to identify them as soon as possible, have you anyone who would go with you?"

Later that day, when Beth felt that she could cry no more, she rang Father Joseph at St. Georges who made the flight bookings and was prepared to go with her. He also spoke to the Cruise Company. Two days later when they were on the flight to Alicante, Beth suddenly said, "How can God do this to me? I try hard to serve Him at the crypt; my parents went to church in the village, were well liked and always gave liberally to the work of the Church. They did not deserve this kind of end."

In years to come Beth remembered the vicar's words. "Beth God does love us all but He has given us all a will of our own-to choose what we do and where we will go, for whatever reason the bus driver lost control your parents put their trust in him and the driver let them down. Very often the people who come to the crypt have chosen to go their own way and hurt many others in their choices, but if we believe in Him, He will bring good out of every situation, although we often have to bear the consequences of other people's wrong doing." He held her hands and prayed for strength to meet whatever situation was before them.

It had been a sad and difficult time. Beth would have been devastated had not Joseph been with her. When they returned to London she went to the rectory, together with Joseph's wife Jane they made lists of the things to be done for the funeral, people who needed to be told, although Beth had few relatives, mainly in Scotland, her cousin who was a vet would certainly come to support her.

Jake, a close friend in London, came to the rectory to see her.

"You must let me come to the farm and work Beth. I was brought up on my father's farm in South Africa and know all about animals. We have been friends for so long working together at the crypt, I want to be there for you," he said sympathetically.

"What about your job in London?" Beth was thinking what a change it would be for him to leave the bright lights of town to settle in the quietness of the countryside. Joseph and Jane thought it would be a good idea, at least to try and see if it worked well. Jake gave in his notice and made his way down to Wales shortly afterwards.

Beth made her way home the following day, frantically arranging the funeral in the village. Her parents had been flown home. Everyone in the village was shocked, her parents were well loved. The ladies insisted on making the refreshments afterwards, which was a great help, they were to be laid to rest in the Church yard where Beth could feel closer to them. The service had been very meaningful, but it did not bring them back and although so many lovely things were said about their kindness to the villagers, there was still the sadness of losing them and knowing her life would never be the same again. Her uncle, auntie and cousin had arrived from Scotland to be with her. Nicholas the vet examined the sheep and cows finding them in good health, whilst her uncle went through the accounts with Ted. Being an accountant was very useful.

Looking back two days after the funeral, Beth wondered how she had managed to come through it all. Everyone had been so kind. Ted and Jean had been a tower of strength, like surrogate parents. Now she had to think where and how Jake was going to fit in.

"What is the next step in your life now, Beth, or is it too soon to ask?" said Jake, bringing a cup of coffee into the lounge.

"I am still in shock, Jake, but somehow I have a peace in my heart about the future, which is so surprising in the circumstances, but I know friends are praying for me. The farm will carry on with Bill, Kate, myself and another farm hand. We do not have a milking herd and apart from the lambing season, the sheep mostly take care of themselves."

"Beth, you know I have given up my job to come and be the other 'hand', don't you want me? I am very fond of you, more so than any girl I have known and we have worked well together in London, so why should we not do so here?" He was rather put out by Beth's attitude.

"Of course I want you, Jake. I think a lot of you, too. We have been close friends for two years, but this is nothing like London, no bright lights, a small village one mile over the hills, not much stimulating company. No soup kitchen and down and outs to look after. The most excitement here is a trip into Swansea, shopping once a week to stock up on food and supplies! The weather can be wonderful and atrocious! Jake, being the farmer's son in South Africa is very different to being a farm hand here. You had servants to do all the menial tasks. Of course I have friends in the village I would introduce you to. The youth club would welcome some new ideas. John Morgan, the vicar would welcome someone to help in the Church, organising house-groups, barn dances, etc." Beth smiled, gently.

"Jake, I have painted the worst picture to you because I don't want you to be unhappy here and regret coming. I intend to work in the community when not needed here, putting my nursing skills into the village when necessary and now make this my home again." Beth was afraid she had put Jake off coming, but he needed to know the downside of things before he made the final choice.

"I am surprised to hear you so enthusiastic to be working for the Church, after God took your parents the way He did," said Jake with some bitterness.

"They are in heaven now Jake. Someone said 'He takes the best first and leaves us all to improve!' Bitterness eats into one like a cancer, I do not want to be like Agnes in the village who lost her husband and drove her only daughter away through her misery. My faith is strong and I am going to carry on here until God tells me what plan He has for my life. I somehow feel He has a plan for me other than looking after sheep and cows. I will wait for Him to tell me." Beth did not feel quite as confident as she sounded; inside it still felt like a knife was being turned, especially when all the things around her reminded of her parents.

She remembered the night before going to London to begin her nurse training her mother had folded her arms around her and said, "You were never as precious to me as you are now." How wonderful to be loved like that, so many at the crypt had never known such parental love. The tears flowed again. The words God spoke to Moses hundreds of years ago came back to her … "Certainly I will be with you wheresoever you go," and with that comforting text she said goodnight to Jake and made her way upstairs to bed. Long into the sleepless night she decided that if Jake wanted to stay after all she had said to him, she would agree to let him.

Beth had given Jake the en suite room which had been her parents. He settled in well and was a great help to Ted on the farm. Life now took on a new pattern. Always an early riser Beth took over the cooking making sure they had a substantial breakfast before starting work. Although Jane, from the village, came in to clean two mornings a week, Beth found the new routine quite difficult at first.

Each morning at 11.30 a.m. the four of them would meet to discuss the business of the day and share out the work which had to be done. Bill and Kate were wonderful to Beth; they always seemed to know when she needed a shoulder to cry on without being told. Bill was a wealth of information, which stock was ready to go to market, when the vet should give injections etc., etc.; the information was recorded each day. Beth cooked the midday meal which they all enjoyed after their meetings. She did the shopping in Swansea once a week, in the Land Rover, but also she did go to the village shop to encourage their trade. And so life settled down into a new routine and all were relatively happy. Beth and Jake often walked over the hills and down to the river, viewing the stock and fences, their easy companionship restored.

"I don't want to tell you really, but seeing that you have asked, perhaps I should. There is some talk in the village about you living at the farm with that Jake and you are not married or even engaged. I know people live together in some parts but not in this village they don't, and what's more your mother would not have agreed with such goings on," she said with feeling. The post mistress was always ready to pass on the latest gossip.

"Oh, Mrs Jones, our relationship is not like that at all, we are very good friends. We worked together in the crypt taking food to the homeless in London and the soup kitchen. When my parents died, seeing that he had been brought up on a farm in South Africa, he felt he would like to give us a hand here. He is a tremendous help to us, if you thought we were living in sin do you think we would come to church? And Jake run the youth club? If your villagers have nothing more to do with their time than gossip about us then I am sorry for them. Perhaps I should put a notice on the church notice board." Beth was really upset to think people were thinking like that.

"No need to take on so, Miss Beth, it is only natural people should take an interest in you, you are well respected and your parents were in this village and I would not have it otherwise. There is a letter for that young man, from South Africa, will you take it for him please?" and with that she turned away to serve another customer.

Beth had a lot to think about on her way home, she thought no one would question her integrity and think they were 'living together'. How she longed for her mother, this would not have happened if she had been there.

As she climbed the hill she met Kate coming down the pathway. "Kate, I have a problem, can I come and see you and Bill after supper tonight?"

"Yes of course you know you are always welcome. Bring Jake, he likes hot chocolate," she was already looking forward to having their company.

"No, I can't do that, this is private. Jake is going down to the youth club to play cricket with the youngsters at 6 o'clock. I do hope the rain will keep off; they get so disappointed if they cannot play. I will come in when he has gone," and with that she went into her own house to make a cup of tea, the cure for all ills.

Jake was cleaning his cricket shoes when she arrived in the kitchen.

"Guess what, Jake, I have something good for you," she said, waving the letter before him.

"Well I guess that is really good to hear from the old folks at home, hope nothing is wrong and they want me to go home, I don't get many letters from them usually."

"Come and have a cup of tea, put your feet up and have a good read, you have not told me much about your family at all, you are a long way from them but at least you know they are there." She made the tea.

"I could not be anywhere better than here when the sun is shining and the birds singing," and with a smile on his face he settled down to read the letter.

After tea, with Jake playing cricket, Beth made her way next door. She felt that she was just getting her life on track after eighteen months of farming, and now an insurmountable problem had occurred.

"Come right in, Beth, we are still in the dining room, just finishing our tea and are all ears!"

Beth repeated what had been said in the post office shop. Their first reaction was to take no notice of gossip. Beth felt otherwise. Being a youth leader, Jake should be an example to the village.

Bill put his arm round Beth and said, "How do you see Jake? Just as a friend or a potential husband?"

"I see him as a very good friend, who I have known and worked with as a brother. There is no romance between us. If there had been a spark surely it would have burst into a flame by now. However, all true marriages begin by good friendship, so I am told, how long were you courting?"

"Three years. But only because we could not afford to get married. My salary was so low as a herdsman and Kate lived in at her work, so we could not save and our parents were not well off, but it was all the better for waiting. The only sadness was that we could not have children after Kate had a bad miscarriage, but we have been so happy on this farm all these years. Your father was like a brother to me; we thought the same and had the same values in life, so we have been truly blessed. Why don't you talk to Jake tonight?"

"I could never ask him to marry me. That would really put him in a spot. If he had any feelings for me he would have said so, however, I will ask him how we sort it out. Marriage would be the best solution. I guess, but would it lead to love automatically?

"Ay, lass, I cannot be sure it would, talk to him and see what he says the answer is but we do not want to lose him."

After more coffee and general chat Beth went home and early to bed.

It was a long sleepless night. Beth lay thinking, wondering what the outcome of the talk she must have with Jake would be. When he had put his arms round her in her sorrow, she had hoped that might be the start of something deeper, but nothing materialised. 'What is wrong with me?' She'd had others interested in her in London, but no real sparks. 'Lord you know me and what I need. If it is Jake's friendship, please make me satisfied with that."

The next morning they were both up bright and early. The sun was shining, the trees in full leaf, the birds singing and having their breakfast. "What have you got on today, Jake?" Beth felt she wanted to get out into the countryside.

"Nothing pressing, we are well on with the extra summer work, why do you want me to do something extra?" he replied.

"No let us have a day out, take a picnic down by the river near the old manor house where I used to play with the children who lived there, Johnathan and Chloe Bryce Jones, they left about six years ago and the lovely old house has been empty since then. I will pack up whilst you tell Bill that we are out for the day, we do not take enough time off. We will 'hold the fort' whilst they have a day off when they like."

Beth felt a bit excited as she took off her jeans and put on a lovely floral skirt a white blouse with a red kerchief to match the skirt, white socks and trainers for walking over the fields.

"Well, you do look a picture and no mistake, no old jeans and sweater today then, is this a special occasion? When are you going to let me in on the secret the suspense is killing me," Jake laughingly told her as he picked up the hamper. They laughed and talked of their London experiences and the people they had helped, in comparison their life here was idyllic but again the thought came to her that cows and animals do not really need her skills but people do. She did help the village midwife when she had too much to do but that was all.

The countryside had never looked better, the grass so green, the conkers beginning to ripen on the trees, wild flowers in the meadows where the cows and sheep grazed contentedly. The verse of a poem came to mind she could not remember from where 'God's in His Heaven all's right with the world', if only it were true. 'Well, Mum and Dad, you are in heaven and my pain is getting a little bit less, thank you Lord.'

"Come on let's sing as we go; what is your favourite song Jake?"

"All things bright and beautiful today, Wales has many purple headed mountains and rivers running by also cold winds in the winter!! But He gave us eyes to see them and lips that we might tell, how great is God almighty who has done all things well, let's sing who will do all things well."

They really enjoyed laughing and singing as they reached the old manor house, feeling carefree in tune with nature and with each other.

The old summer house was looking dilapidated, it had seen better days. "This was our den," Beth said. "We imagined it was sometimes a ship sailing up the Amazon or Nile, at other times a castle with the enemy coming up the river, we had vivid imaginations often sleeping in the woods on warm summer nights, it is so far off the beaten track not many people knew it was here."

They then walked round the outside of the house looking through the windows where some of the furniture still was in place and suddenly in the quietness she felt God speaking to her, giving a picture of children running around the garden as she used to do, of people coming to this lovely place to find peace and healing, of the place coming alive again all for the glory of God. The Peace she felt was just so wonderful, the presence of the Holy Spirit around her gave her such joy she knew then what God had got for her to do, "Lord," she said, "I will do this with your help show me the way to make this a home of rest and healing here."

Jake was laying out the rug on the river bank, Beth was very quiet she had to talk to Jake but she could not tell him what she felt God had said to her just yet.

She was very apprehensive as they ate their picnic. "Come on, Beth I know you have something to say, spill the beans, have I done something wrong boss?"

"First of all I am not your boss, we are in the farm together along with the Jacksons, but I have to say something which is worrying me." Beth took a deep breath and told him then what the people in the village were saying. He was silent for a long time thinking what to say; when he spoke it was with hesitation.

"I have wondered how long it would be before they came up with this, they do not believe two people can live in the same house without sex; I am afraid it is the way of the world. What do you want me to do, Beth? Shall I move out and get another job?"

"Oh no, Jake, I don't want to lose you, you have been such a great help to me in so many ways, not only on the farm but a real companion as well. The only other way is to stay here and marry me, oh dear, what have I said; I have now embarrassed you. I know you are not attracted to me physically, but it would be a marriage of convenience, would that would be enough to begin with?" Beth was mortified by what she had just said.

Jake took his time in replying, "I can see that one day you will meet some chap you really love and then you would be hampered with me, but it is one way of solving the problem. But is a marriage of convenience enough for you, Beth? I do love you, Beth, but I am not 'in love with you' as a man should be, I must be honest with you."

"That surly is enough to start with, love does grow and marriage starts with good friendship, so I am told, but I would hate the villagers to think they had forced us into it."

Beth was disappointed by Jake's reaction to her proposal. "What is wrong with me?" she asked Kate the next day.

There is nothing wrong with you, my love, you are so attractive in many ways, warm hearted, kindness itself, very hospitable to all you entertain here and in the village, you have a lovely smile you are not short of admirers that I can tell you. You do not know much about Jake's life in South Africa or of his relationship with his parents. Sometimes this can get in the way; if his parents were not happy with each other and he is afraid the same thing might happen to him." She was sad for Beth because she thought she really loved Jake.

There had been an awkwardness between them on the way home yesterday from the picnic which had not gone away at breakfast time the next morning.

"I am thinking about our conversation of yesterday, Beth, and trying to work things out. We will have another chat tonight after supper and come to a conclusion one way or another." With that he went out to see to the animals and collect the eggs, obviously confused!

Beth had forgotten that night she and Kate went to the village to the keep fit class; a girls together evening. There was a lot of good company there; laughter and leg pulling after the class was finished. As they chatted they were invited to the Barn Dance on Saturday night.

"Bring your husbands and any spare men you can pick up on the way, we are always short of men at these do's."

"I have not got a husband yet but will ask Jake to come; it is a pity sheep won't do I could bring plenty of them!" Beth laughingly said.

"Come on, Beth, time to go home, see you all on Saturday, do you want any cooking doing for the refreshments afterwards?"

"Oh yeah, please, we always enjoy your cakes and sausage rolls," and with that they went on their way home.

Beth and Kate sat in the car chatting outside the house. Please let us pray about the discussion Jake and I are having later; that the outcome will be God's will for our lives. We do need His guidance."

Jake was in his room when Beth went into the house. He did not offer to come down for the chat. Not a good omen for a prospective bridegroom! He casually called goodnight when he heard her open her bedroom door, She sat at her desk for a long time trying to sort out her true feelings and praying that that Lord would give her the answer through Jake telling her what he wanted to do the next day.

Jake was up the next morning with the breakfast ready before 6.30 a.m. It was market day and some of the cows were going to be sold. They had to be loaded into the cattle truck with Bill's help whilst Beth made sandwiches and a flask for their lunch. She used to be so sad as a child when the cows went to be sold because she gave them names and looked on them as friends!

"It was too late last night when you came in to have our chat, but I have decided that we can be married as long as you are satisfied with a marriage of convenience and we go on as we have done these past two or three years. We are good mates we live and work well together, so there should not be too many problems. Think about the arrangements to be made, I think it should be soon." With that he picked up his lunch box and went on his way.

Autumn was well on its way, the leaves were beginning to turn into lovely shades of gold and tan. Kate with Beth set out after lunch with containers to pick blackberries down the hedges around the farm. The orchard was shedding the loads of apples and pears which grew there, far more than they needed, so she organised a "picking" party for those in church who wanted to come and help themselves for the next Sunday afternoon and was to give them tea afterwards.

As they arrived home with so much fruit Kate started the jam making process straight away. Beth went into the orchard to the Bramley Apple tree that she had planted when she was a little girl hardly strong enough to hold the small spade to fill in the earth around it, her parents had laughed at her. Now she put her arms round the trunk and sobbed uncontrollably." Mum and Dad how I miss you", suddenly she felt their presence very close to her, "please help me to make the right decisions for my life, I long to be as happy in married life as you were, I will make these pies and jam just as we used to do, Mum, and take them to the folks in the village to carry on your tradition."

It was quite late in the day when Jake and Bill came home from market. The day had gone well, all the cattle sold for good prices. Beth had made a meat and potato pie for them all with blackberry and apple pie with cream to follow. After a long chat about the day in the market Bill and Kate made their way home.

Seated in the lounge with a cup of coffee Jake brought up the subject of the wedding." I will marry you, Beth, because I do love you but not the same kind of love a bridegroom normally has for his bride. I am not sure there will be children, the physical side will be difficult, I can't be more specific than that, but, we can go on as we are now only as Mr and Mrs to the world outside. Will that be enough for you?"

"Jake, my dearest friend, our love will be all that deeper than the sexual stuff people go on about; I am sure that will be enough. When will the wedding be? Will there be enough time to get the wedding invitations out to our London friends and your family in South Africa?"

"No I think they will not want to come all this way to a quiet wedding. You mentioned the church wedding but I do not want that I want a registry office ceremony and perhaps a blessing in church at the morning service. I can't make vows before God that I maybe cannot keep. It is a wedding of convenience after all not quite the same. Will you ring your cousin tonight?" Jake seemed quite adamant about what he wanted.

"Oh, Jake, what has happened to us, we are not the same as we were last week, happy and care free, if this is upsetting you then it is not going to happen," Beth was almost in tears.

"Yes it is, Beth, it is what you wanted, there is no reason it should be any different to what we are now. Actually we could slip off to the registry office with Bill and Kate any time and have a meal afterwards, somewhere nice it would save a lot of trouble."

Beth was quite devastated by his attitude with unwelcome tears in her eyes she cried out, "I want this marriage to mean something to us, to put God in the centre of our relationship otherwise it will fail," she had never doubted Jake until this moment but it seemed the only way to go with his wishes if they were going to carry on living together, she did not want to lose him, he was a good worker on the farm and had been a good companion.

"We will ask the vicar if he will bless us after the morning service and we will provide refreshments afterwards," Beth was coming to terms with the idea of a registry office wedding and a blessing afterwards when the friends from church could celebrate with them.

The next morning Jake was busy with the telephone directory looking for the number to ring the Registry office. He got out his diary to look for dates when they could be away from the farm; it seemed the date could be three weeks away. Poor Beth seemed as if she had no part in these arrangements, this was a new Jake; he usually left the decision making to her being so easy going himself.

When Bill and Kate came in later in the morning to discuss the farm work, Beth said she had some news for them. We are celebrating! Today we are getting married in three weeks' time in Swansea and would like you two to be our witnesses please. After all you are my surrogate parents and I need your support. This is to be a marriage of convenience, not quite a conventional one, but we are asking the vicar if he will give us a blessing after the morning service the week after and I will provide the refreshments afterwards." It all came out in a rush!

There was a stunned silence. Beth looked at them worriedly, "Well are you not pleased for us, it will at least stop the village tongues wagging?"

"That is no reason to get wed for without love and commitment it will surly fail," Bill was clearly upset by this news, Kate as well; she went to make the coffee to escape Beth's serious face.

"Bill we do love each other, have known each other for four years and lived here for two, nothing will change only my name and status!" Beth was disappointed at their reaction but was sure they would come round before long. "We could get engaged at the barn dance on Saturday what do you think? You could get the ring after the market tomorrow Jake, perhaps Kate and I could go with you to do some shopping?

It was a very sober couple who went to their home for dinner "there is something not right about them marrying, Kate. If they had intended tying the knot why had it taken village gossips to make their minds up?"

"Beth is very fond of him, Bill, has been for a long time. I just hope she is going to be happy and not making a big mistake."

Beth and Kate went shopping for wedding clothes whilst the men were at the market. Beth chose a cream lace dress ankle length over a pale pink satin under slip, with pink shoes and a skull cap of silk pink flowers to match her gloves. Kate had a deeper pink dress and jacket with white shoes and gloves to match. They really enjoyed the morning and passing a jeweller's shop, Kate said, "I might as well buy the rings, Jake will not have time to get them after we meet them." And with that they went and chose a pretty ring, a circle of diamonds which was to be her wedding ring, which Beth paid for.

This is all wrong, thought Kate, but for Beth's sake she went along with it. "We can wear these things for the blessing in Church, Kate; it will be lovely to get dressed up out of working clothes and show the villagers we are attractive ladies in spite of our work."

Beth went to see the vicar with Jake the next day they were honest with him telling him the real reason in confidence for their wedding. He was not entirely happy about it. "We do love each other, vicar, and we do not want people thinking we live together; this seems to be the only way out of the situation."

All continued to be well with the farm. The accountant came every month to see the figures complimenting Beth on the way the accounts were kept and the movement of the livestock, to say nothing of the sale of eggs and vegetables which she and Bill cultivated selling to a ready market in the village. He was amazed that she had picked bookkeeping up so easily although she was nurse trained. She paid Bill handsomely for being the manager also Jake was on to a good thing as well! They were running the stock down as winter was just around the corner; last year was a good winter, not much snow, but usually being on top of a hill the snow, when it came, drifted deeply around the houses. There had always been very large barns for keeping the cattle and sheep in should the weather be very bad, her father and grandfather had most carefully cared for the animals always storing plenty of feed in case of bad weather. After Christmas when the lambs were born many nights were spent in the sheep barn, which, in spite of being on the hill, was fairly cosy and warm. Beth had never envisaged being a midwife to the sheep! But she did enjoy bringing new life into the world, even lambs.

The day of the wedding arrived. Beth's nerves were strained, Jake was no blushing bridegroom. Only twice had he 'pecked' at her cheek, no loving kisses, but maybe that would change after today. The cooking for the nest day's blessing had all been done and was in the freezer, cooked hams beef salads, etc. Her relatives had come from Scotland the only guests at the registry office apart from Kate and Bill.

Beth had to admit to herself she had some misgivings, after breakfast she went to her room and spent a long time in prayer. Strangely enough she remembered how Jesus felt before He went to the cross. He knew the awful death was before Him … He was to be the Saviour of all mankind, to bear their sin, to die on the cross, He prayed for his tormentors as He went forward. Why should she be thinking of this on her wedding day? She prayed for Jake and herself that they would become a truly happy couple and continue to help other people as they had done in London,

Looking back it had all gone extremely well; the registry office was a cold ceremony very quickly over, a notice saying that it was a legal transaction on the wall reminded her that this was not a sacred ceremony. However the next day was a different story! The morning service was a very joyful one. The sermon was on the water being turned into wine at the wedding Jesus and his Mother went to, when the wine ran out and Jesus performed a miracle. The real meaning of the story the vicar said was that Jesus took ordinary things in life and made them special, who would have thought of Jesus being concerned about what the couple felt like running out of wine? How often in life do we 'run out of wine? Come to the end of our own resources and need God's help in the common things we do each day. Beth said a fervent amen to that. After the blessing, there had been dark clouds in her life and there would be again, but He would see her through. Little did she know what lay ahead in life for her.

The friends from the village all came to the church and reception. They complimented them on their lovely clothes, they had never seen Jake wearing a suit before and probably wouldn't again! After all the well wishes and real love shown to them Beth made her way alone to her parents grave to lay her flowers there, she told them what had happened although she knew they were in heaven but hoped they somehow knew.

Kate cooked a meal for them all at her house that evening; the talk was mainly about the farm and the future of it. No one was thrilled about the coming winter, the snow and wintery weather was almost worse in Wales. Jake was asked about his life in sunny South Africa, working with his father on their farm but was almost reluctant to speak about his years as a child.

Uncle John and Kenneth stayed for several days before going home. Beth took them for a walk by the river the next day. "It was so good to have you this weekend, uncle, you are so much like Daddy I almost thought he was there."

"Beth, tell me one thing which has puzzled us both, why did you not get married in church instead of the Registry office?" He was genuinely perplexed.

Beth then told them the real reason they had decided to get married, seeing that they were concerned.

"Does Jake know that you are a very rich woman, Beth?

"No he knows nothing of my inheritance only that I own the farm. I do not think he married me for my money Uncle, we have been close friends for almost three years in London before Mummy and Daddy died. He offered to come and work here on the farm I did not ask him to, in fact I tried to put him off thinking a quiet life in Wales was very different to the one we had lived in London, but nothing would have put him off, He has been a tremendous help, very hard working, I could not have done without him, especially in the home, although we have the two dogs in the house when Jake is there I am not afraid of intruders. We have always had separate rooms, I'm afraid there is no romance between us, but that is how we like it," replied Beth

"Oh Beth you may not always feel like that; a lovely girl like you should have more out of a marriage than companionship at your age. Promise me you will always share your problems with me should any arise in the future and do not tell him about your financial affairs in the foreseeable future, I like the chap but there is just something I am not quite sure about. Don't worry about what I have said perhaps I should have kept it to myself." He then was sorry that he had been so forthright. As they walked by the river, the old manor house came into view, "This is a lovely old house, Beth, do you know who owns it? What a shame it has been left to run down."

"I do know the owners and spent very many happy hours playing here as a child. There were two children here about my age and we were almost inseparable. We had so many happy days here camping in the woods, fishing and generally running wild. My parents would have been surprised at the things we got up to. Go and look inside through the windows a lot of the original furniture is still there, although it is six years since they left. Mr. Bryce Jones had dementia in the end and after the children had left home his wife could not cope with him, so Mummy said. Actually I do not think there was much love lost between them, there were many quarrels between them and she could not stand the children around her that's why we had such a good time avoiding her! I will let you in to a very big secret, I am hoping to buy this house when it comes up for sale and make it into a home where children and people can come from London for holidays here. Jake and I used to work in the crypt giving out soup and dinners to those who had nothing. I believe that is what God wants me to do with my life, not feed sheep and cows forever!"

"Well good for you, Beth; that is a wonderful idea, what does Jake think to that?"

"He does not know and I do not want him to just yet, it is a pipe dream at the moment but I really think God is going to bring it to pass in His good time. No-one but you knows anything so please keep it to yourself and Kenneth. "I would sell the farm, but keep several fields around the manor to build on and make playing fields, etc. This venture is still at the prayer stage and will be for some time then I will share it with Bill and Kate and am sure they will want to come in on it with me, if not other arrangements can be made for the new owner to keep him on as farm manager. If they want to come I will build them a bungalow next to the house."

"Well Kate you have it all worked out and if it happens you can count on my help in selling the farm."

"If God wants it to happen then it will and I am content to wait His time."

They resumed their walk by the river up through the fields through masses of fallen leaves. It really looked like autumn now; the hazel nuts and chestnuts were falling giving the village children many happy hours collecting them. They say every season has its own beauty, but bare branches never thrilled Beth, she had to think if the leaves did not come off the new shoots would not be able to come through in the spring time.

Whilst they were away Kenneth once again was looking over the sheep and cows, it was handy having a vet in the family; the sad thing was he was far away in Scotland. Beth made a big farewell dinner that night with Bill and Kate. It did not seem right to be eating one of their sheep but it was delicious with apple and blackberry pie to follow and lots of cream. In the kitchen Kenneth put his arm round Beth and said, "You work too hard, darling, I know you have help but your parents would be so pleased that you have taken to farming so well."

"They just wished I had been a boy; I am sure is nice to be called darling again. Daddy used to call me that," she said wistfully.

There were only the two of them in the kitchen he put his arm round her and said "Married life is not easy; Fay and I live almost separate lives and yet we love one another, we have different temperaments, but have come to accept that in ten years. If ever you need a friend please ring if only to say you are OK. Promise?" he leaned over and kissed her, she wished that was Jake's kiss.

Early the next morning Beth took them down to Swansea station to catch their train to London, and then the night sleeper to Edinburgh.

"It has been great having you with us, please come again and bring Fay with you. It is a long way but you could always fly to Cardiff we could meet you there." Beth felt almost tearful saying good bye.

"Bring Jake up to us for a holiday. I don't think he is too keen on me, I just get that feeling, but come alone if not."

"Here's the train ... bye darlings, safe journey," Beth waved until they were out of sight.

After dinner that night Jake and Beth were sitting by the fire when she said, "Jake we must decide which room we are going to use now that we are married. There is a double bed in my room and also in yours so which will you choose?"

"I do not want you in my bed, Beth, I like sleeping alone and do not intend sharing with anyone. We carry on as normal. Beth have you forgotten already?" he said very pointedly.

Beth was quite speechless; she was so hurt at the tone of his voice, her cheeks were flaming in embarrassment, she stood up to go out with the dogs so he would not notice. She walked around the garden and sat on the seat in the memorial garden she had made in memory of her parents welcoming the cold air as it cooled her cheeks. Bill, looking out of the bedroom window at the lovely moon shining on the duck pond, saw her and guessed what had happened. Jake had changed since the wedding, he was no longer the happy go lucky chap he used to be, but looked as if he was in a world of his own, always something on his mind. Not wanting their friends in London to come to the wedding, not even telling his parents he was married; was he hiding something? He was glad to share his thoughts with Kate before going to sleep.

Early in December the snow came, it gave them time to round up the animals and get then into the barn under cover. For the next two months all over Christmas the snow came and then the thaw followed by more snow until the roads were impassable on many occasions. The four of them were marooned most of the time at the farm house. Their own milking cow gave them plenty of milk and Beth was able to make cream and even some butter. They had plenty of feed for the stock but no market days. The barns had to be mucked out regularly which did not improve Jake's moods! He had grown very introverted, he had a wood carving hobby which he had plenty of time to do; he made wooden animals, walking sticks, etc., being quite clever and creative. Beth knitted and sewed as did Kate next door. Christmas came and went with more snow. The television was their comfort at this time, they did not feel quite so cut off enjoying the films and documentaries.

January saw the preparation of the lambing season.

All the equipment for hot drinks and snacks to see the midwives through the long nights! They worked out a duty rota which worked out very well most of the time. This went on for several weeks. During this time Beth had an invitation from a friend from the hospital to go to Switzerland to a nurses' Christian Conference at Easter time for five days. Beth was worried that they could not do without her, but Kate insisted that she should go. Bill had a nephew who was an agriculture student at a London university who was needing a placement on a farm for two months. Kate was delighted to have him work there with them, so it was settled that she should go.

Jake was very quiet about her going, he was very subdued, quiet and almost morose. The work on the farm went well that winter more lambs than before survived being born in the barn. As soon as the cold winds eased off the sheep and lambs were put into the fields and looked a pretty sight.

Whilst walking to the village post office Beth came across old Tom leaning on the gate looking at the sheep. Tom used to work for Beth's father in his younger days always a favourite with a smile on his face. "Good morning, Miss Beth, these lambs are a real treat to the eyes and so are you if I might say so, I said to my wife at your wedding, I've known her all her life and there is no better person living, she is lovely inside and out!"

"Go on you old flatterer, have you been to the optician's lately to have your eyes tested? It's good to talk to you. I don't often get a compliment, so cheerio I am going to the post office."

After dinner that night when it was time for bed, Beth put on her best pretty night dress after bathing in rose water and smelling nice; she thought she would have another try to get into Jake's bed!! She waited until he was in bed and slid in beside him.

"What are you doing, Beth? He was really angry and jumped out of the other side, "This was not our agreement, remember, a marriage of convenience, please go to your own bed."

"I just needed to feel your arms around me, nothing else, Jake, is it really too much for me to ask? I shall be going away at the weekend and would like to think you will miss me other than for making your meals."

"You know what we agreed and I have kept to what I said at the time. You never ask for any money for my board, but I know you are pretty well off; we have never discussed money because I do not know your financial affairs. This farm alone is worth a fortune, if ever you sell, which I don't expect that cousin of yours would agree to. I am not going to fall out with you, Beth so please go to your own room to bed," he was clearly put out about something.

Beth went down to make some hot chocolate and took her favourite dog upstairs with her. At least cuddling the dog was better than a husband who did not want her. Instead of sleep she made a list of things to take with her on Saturday and began to look forward to seeing her old friends again. 'Lord this marriage is not working out as I had hoped, please sort it out for me,' she silently prayed.

The next morning Jake was all sweetness and light." I have to go to a hill farm ten miles away to collect some lambs, Bill and I decided to restock after we narrowed our stock before the winter. Would you like to come with me? We could have a pub lunch before picking them up."

"Yes indeed I would love to come, I will be ready when you come in for coffee." Beth was joyful; after last night she did not expect a trip out today. She put on her smartest jeans with a white polo jumper, a pretty scarf round her neck and felt good about herself. They took the small cattle trailer chatting amicably all the way. The lunch at the pub called the Sheep and Shepherd, well named for the hill farmers, was most enjoyable, so, too, was the tea the farmer's wife gave Beth in their sitting room whist the lambs were being loaded. They had enjoyed their day out and given them both something to remember in the days ahead.

All too soon it was Saturday morning. Jake was taking Beth to the London train around 8.30 a.m. Peter the nephew was installed at the farm living with Bill and Kate. A very cheerful lad full of fun being so pleased to be working there and no doubt would be a great hit with the girls in the village!

"Would you like to be coming Jake? "She asked him.

"What with three women? No thank you. Perhaps I will take a holiday this year myself, climbing in Scotland or something like that."

"We could both go and stay with Uncle, he would love us to do that," said Beth eagerly.

"No thanks, Beth, I would go alone." Climbing is not your scene and I do enjoy my own company."

"Well you are going to have some this week, Peter is a nice lad but he is next door, I think he would stay with you if you asked him," she replied.

"I do not want that," Jake said with feeling. "Here is the train, Beth, have a lovely time, you will be back when?"

"Next Saturday; I shall visit Father Joseph for three days whilst in London." He lifted the case in the train, gave her the briefest kiss on the cheek, slammed the door and she was off.

Beth felt a feeling of exhilaration as the train gathered speed, she felt her cares and worries slip away and for the next week she was going to forget about the farm and Jake and come closer to God by the friendship and meetings they were going to have. People from different countries and denominations all in one meeting together, it should be a foretaste of heaven, she thought. Jane and Mary met her in London and after a late lunch they made their way to Heathrow Airport for the evening flight to Switzerland.

As they waited for the flight together, they reminisced about when they had been in training at the London Hospital they had started a group called the Hospital Christian fellowship and met regularly, when duty would allow, to sing and pray together. Sometimes they had a speaker who would give them words of encouragement. Nursing was hard work, not only physically but emotionally as well. There were times when they had prayed for a patient to be healed and it had not happened physically, but hopefully by their prayers the patients had a peaceful end. Many times in the meetings there were tears, but they helped one another through these difficult times.

The four days at the conference went all too quickly and they were back in London feeling refreshed and Beth looked forward to meeting Father Joseph and his lovely wife again; being in the Church of England they were allowed to marry.

Father Joseph asked Beth about her marriage to Jake; he was concerned that she had never contacted him before the wedding. She explained to him that Jake arranged the wedding and did not want any friends there as it was a marriage of convenience therefore he did not see it as a 'proper marriage'.

"And how has it been since, Beth? A proper marriage consummated?"

"No it has not, but we are good friends and that is how it has to be; perhaps better than nothing."

"I have a friend who is a gynaecologist. I think he should examine you, Beth. You might need evidence one day. I have known Jake for a long time, longer than you, and he just might have ulterior motives about this marriage, he knows you are 'well off' and he could want this to work for his advantage. Has he told you about his past life in South Africa?

"Oh I don't think that for one minute, I suggested the wedding to stop the people thinking we were living together. No, I haven't heard much about his parents, as far as I know he has only had two letters from them!" she replied.

"Beth, I am always here if you should need me in the future, we still help all the folks we can in the east end as well as the crypt. A lot of them now come to church and have found a new life, some going back home to be united with their families; others, with our help, finding places to live and work. So we feel very rewarded." The priest was very fond of Beth and did not want her to be hurt.

Beth told him about the Manor project she had in mind. "When I get home that is the first thing I will share with Jake and find out if they are willing to sell. I can afford to pay for the manor house before I sell the farm, afterwards to do the necessary alterations to house for the people you are going to send me for holidays, and peace of mind." It was good to share this vision finding an enthusiastic partner. .

Keep me informed, Beth, but be careful how much you tell Jake about your finances.

Beth trusted Father Joseph, so she had an examination before going home on the Saturday. She did feel the priest had been hard on Jake. Although he had been awkward about the wedding and withdrawn at times in the beginning, he was more pleasant and she thought he was happy. She did not know what he was going to say about the Manor project or what Bill and Kate would say; it was going to affect them all. Beth was thirty years old and if she was not going to have children she did not want to spend the whole of her life looking after the farm, much as she loved her old home. 'Dear Lord please make it happen for your glory.'

When Beth arrived at Swansea station later that night she eagerly looked along the platform for the sight of Jake but he was not there. He must have been held up, so taking her case she went into the waiting room. After waiting a quarter of an hour she heard her name on the Tannoy asking her to go to the enquiries desk where she found her car keys attached to a card bearing her name. The attendant told her that a young man had left them yesterday saying he could not meet her as he had been called away.

Mystified, Beth found her car and started for home. Kate was waiting for her outside as soon as she heard the car coming up the hill to the house. Beth jumped out into her welcoming arms and into the kitchen for that welcome cup of tea.

"What is going on Kate? Where is Jake? Why was he not at the station?"

"Beth, I don't know. We have hardly seen him this week whilst you have been away. Yesterday we saw him with a case and backpack getting into your car. He did not speak to us, just waved his hand and drove down the hill."

"I guess he has gone to Scotland for the walking holiday he talked about," said Kate not a bit perturbed.

"You will stay for dinner? We are just ready to dish up. We have missed you, Beth, and are longing to hear how the Conference went, and also the trip to your London friends"

Beth talked on for the next hour then said good night and went into her own empty house accompanied by Bill. They went into the kitchen and propped on the mantel piece was a letter addressed to Beth.

"I will leave you to your love letter," joked Bill. "We are only next door if you need us."

'Dear Beth,' the letter said. 'If you are not doing so please sit down as what I have to say to you will come as a bit of a shock to you. I am sorry that I am so much of a coward and cannot say this to your face, in spite of this I do still have some feelings for you and hate hurting you. Whilst our relationship was friends we got along very well, because of what others thought we ruined that by getting married. I should have told you a long time ago.

'I thought by getting married I might change, but unfortunately that has not happened. I am not and never have been a practicing "gay" person but am easier with men's company than ladies. My parents discovered this when their efforts to get me married to various lovely girls failed; they guessed something was wrong with me. They disowned me and threw me out, wanted no more to do with me, that is why I do not talk about them, it is still after all these years very painful. I came to London and lived in a hostel and then found the crypt, Father Joseph and you. After a while I got work in an accounts office and secretly battled with my feelings. Father Joseph toiled many hours with me in prayer and counselling, because of this I, to a certain extent, got rid of all my feelings and enjoyed your company. Buried in Wales I had no problems until our marriage, especially the night you came to my bed. I saw the hurt in your eyes and hated myself for putting you through this sham, but still could not tell you. I have never had a relationship with anyone, male or female, but I love you dearly as a brother The final straw was when Peter came to the farm, he is such a super lad and I just could not trust myself and realised I must release you to find true love and a family with someone else, which I cannot give you. I long to be different. I have sought help but it has not been permanent. I am hoping to travel the world working my way round so don't try and find me. My solicitor will be in touch releasing you from our marriage. Anything you want to say to me can be done through the solicitor. I shall not be sorry to leave England, the cold winter just passed nearly finished me off! Thank you, dear Beth, for all you have done for me and given me, believe me if it could have been different I would have been so happy with you my lovely friend and companion. God bless you … my love for what it is worth. Jake.'

With a stifled cry of anguish she rushed into Kate's house and gave them the letter. She felt drained inside and frozen. All kinds of thoughts whizzing through her mind, why had she not guessed this was the problem? It all added up, although he certainly never looked at any fellow in that way. She blamed herself for proposing to him. Dear Lord please help me over this one, I am devastated, where do I go from here? Straight away a voice said to her, "To the Manor."

Of course Kate and Bill were so surprised by the letter, "It is better that you find out now, Beth, and can sort yourself out. I am sure God has had His hand in this. The Bible says 'all things work together for good for those who put their trust in Him and are called to work for Him'."

Beth rang Kenneth in Scotland with the news the next morning. He was not surprised and had guessed what the problem was when they did not sleep together on their wedding night.

The next person she rang was Father Joseph who was almost expecting the call. He could not tell her when she stayed with them because of confidentiality. "What can I tell the Vicar here and the villagers, a bridegroom of six months leaving without a word to the boys club, certainly not the real cause of the marriage break up?"

Kate encouraged her to go to Father Joseph for a while so two days later she boarded the train again. Yes they had seen Jake at the rectory on the Sunday and later that night he had flown to Canada where he had a cousin on a ranch who would give him work to start with. He told Father Joseph he had all his wages saved up because Beth never charged him to live there, so he had a good bank account and would not be destitute.

Beth arrived home with a much lighter heart; straight away she took the dogs and walked down to the Manor beside the river. To her surprise there was a 'For sale' notice up with a phone number to ring, the estate agent was in Swansea and she could not get home fast enough to ring them.

Later that evening she called Kate, Bill and Peter in for coffee and to ask them what they thought about the Manor project. The estate agent was coming round the next morning to see the inside of the property, although she knew that better than he did!

Beth outlined her vision for the Manor asking how they felt about coming in with her, Bill to see to the very reduced cattle numbers, enough for the children who had never seen animals and where the milk came from, etc. And Kate to be the cook, with help of course.

"The other alternative is for me to sell the farm with you as manager, Bill, that way nothing would change. If you came in with me I would build you a bungalow near the house so that you could be private if you so wished."

Beth was surprised at the enthusiasm with which they talked about the project. They said they had wondered what the future held for them because Beth would not want to bury herself forever more at the farm. It would be different if she had a family but now she had not got a husband!!

The next morning they all went with the estate agent for the Manor. Beth thought the asking price was` very reasonable because it was very run down and also out of the way. There was only an unmade road up to and passed the house into the woods, only hikers and fishermen used the path which suited Beth very well. The river flowed past the house and the banks were covered in early spring flowers.

"The fields down to the house belong to us, also the woodland along the river bank, we will not sell them because we will extend the buildings at the back and build barns to house the animals ... and who knows what else? Three very excited people went back up the hill back for lunch. Peter came in and asked where he came into the picture. Peter was Bill's nephew who was studying at the Agricultural College and had come to help on the farm whilst Beth was in Switzerland. "You can come and do whatever you like, Peter, there will always be a place for you." she was glad of his interest. The estate agent put the farm up for sale immediately and they had several enquiries over the next few weeks.

Beth went into the village to see the vicar to tell him of her plans also to pray about the new venture. He suggested that on Sunday morning she should outline her plans to the congregation and get their support. Not everyone will welcome it, she felt, but the youth club would, they missed Jake and it would be an opportunity to tell them he was working around the world because he always wanted to do that, also the last winter 'got to him' as he was South African and was used to the sun. Her news was generally well received, explaining the visitors would be spending money in the village and any enterprising person might set up a business selling sailable goods which people and visitors would be tempted to buy.

Chapter 2

The move down to The Alpha Home was scheduled for the first day of June. Although the sale of the farm was not completed Beth agreed to the new manager moving into the house whilst Bill was still living in the house next door. Beth was very excited but also sad to be leaving her childhood home. Julie and Kate were going with her, their rooms were already decorated and furnished to their own choice, although Kate would be moving out when her bungalow was built. Peter asked if he could come down and help during the summer at least, he was staying with Bill.

It seemed very strange cooking a supper of scrambled eggs in the new kitchen, everything shiny and new. Before going to bed Beth stood by the river outside the front door loving the sounds of the birds settling for the night; a blackbird was singing in the quietness as the sun went down. A rabbit hopped across the pathway into a hole on the river bank. A saying came into her mind, she could not remember from where 'God's in His Heaven, all's right with the world', If only that was true!

The next morning Peter was down bright and early "It isn't hard to get up early here, Beth, I would still be in bed at home. What do I do today?"

"We need some furniture moving and the garden layout put on paper. I guess you are good at garden planning, after lunch we will get together and I will show you what I have in mind. Beth took the Land Rover into the cash and carry in Swansea. She stocked up the store room with all they would need in groceries and cleaning materials also spades forks, etc., for the gardening. It had been a happy day; Kate had cooked a lovely evening meal and they sat round the kitchen table talking about what was going to happen next month at the official opening.

Julie was rubbing her stomach.

"What is wrong, Julie, have you got a pain or are you just uncomfortable?" Beth enquired.

"I think it is a small pain but nothing to worry about I will go and lie down I have another two weeks to go yet so don't worry, Beth," and with that she made to leave the kitchen.

"Aye, Julie, I told you not to help to move that furniture and stuff upstairs, do you think you have hurt yourself?" Peter was now concerned.

"No, silly, I know you moaned at me but I am OK."

Peter and Beth walked round the woodland path before turning in for the night.

"This is the best part of the day," said Beth. "I had better check on Julie before going to bed, she just might be coming into labour, it would be nice if she were to get it over before the opening," Beth replied.

"Beth, she told me today she is really scared could I stay down here tonight in case I am needed?" said Peter.

"Why, what could you do?"

"I have delivered cows and sheep on my course and always get excited when new life comes into the world no matter who is responsible or caused it to happen."

Beth laughed and laughed, "Julie would be happy if she could hear you likening her to animals!! Well don't forget I am a midwife and she has been seen by the local midwife so I think we are well covered, but I will bear it in mind! Laughingly they went into the house and found Kate looking severe.

43

"I think she is starting in labour, Beth, the pains are more frequent and acute."

After examining Julie, Beth rang the midwife only to be told she was out on another case eight miles away, but they would let her know if she was needed. Beth knew the midwife would leave her to do the delivery if she could not get there; she had helped out many times when there had been two births at the same time.

By eleven o'clock Julie was getting on with her labour. Still very frightened she asked if Peter could sit with her, they had become good friends in the two weeks they had been helping at the home. It rather amused Beth to see and hear Peter encouraging her to hold on, shout, squeeze his hand and anything which would give her some relief.

Beth rang the doctor. I am Beth from the Manor House and I have a seventeen year old girl in the second stage of labour. The midwife who is looking after her is out on another case. I am a midwife and will do the delivery if you so wish. There seem to be no complications at the moment, the heart beat is good and it is in position to be born."

"Why have you rung me at this hour? I am a very busy person just get on with it will you!"

"Well of all the rude men he takes the biscuit," Beth said under her breath. "You might be busy but you are still the doctor on call for this village. Good bye."

Kate was hopping round with hot water, towels, baby clothes, and all the equipment needed for a new birth. The little boy was born at four o'clock in the morning yelling his head off.

Peter said, "Julie, he's taking after you already, he heard you yelling before he was born!!"

"Hot chocolate to celebrate." Kate brought the drinks and chocolate biscuits up after they had washed the baby and put him in Julie's arms.

"You should be feeding him, Julie, all the lambs look for the nipple as soon as they are born," giggled Peter.

"Well I am not a sheep do you want to hold him?"

"Well considering what I have gone through this night I feel like his father. Incidentally, do you think his father should know he has a son?"

"Peter I am so ashamed to tell you that I do not know who his father is. I went to a friend's party from school against my parents' wishes, there was plenty of drink I had not tasted before and in the morning I found myself in my friend's bed with no clothes on. You can understand my parents disowning me and turning me out." She had now told Peter feeling he would not have befriended her had he have known, but instead of that he said, "Well if he has not got a father I guess I had better be one to him."

Julie could not believe her ears. "Well that would be super if you could, but you will not remember in the morning." She turned over and went to sleep if only, Peter meant it; she did like him so much.

The next morning Beth was helping Julie to wash when a voice called up the stairs, "May I come up? Where are you in this mausoleum?"

"Well," said Beth. "You might be the new doctor but you have a lot to learn about civility, you may be used to people having babies by the roadside, but here we are more civilized and have them on the bed with possibly a doctor in attendance."

"Goodness me you are a fire ball, you coped very well without me and here is the result, a super bouncing boy and how is the mother? Julie I think? Is that the proud father I saw downstairs? Come on, old chap, let me have a look at you and see all your bits and pieces. Is he feeding well?"

"He has got off to a good start," Julie said. "And I am feeling very well this morning. I had such good attention and a natural birth, with loving good friends around me. It could not have been better."

"So glad to hear it, you are looking very happy, I will examine you."

"I am not smiling at you but so amused to hear Beth talking to you like I have never heard her speak to any one before!" Julie was enjoying this.

"Sister Beth, we seem to have got off on the wrong foot. I have worked in Africa researching AIDS on a five year programme. I visited the same people every six months living in awful conditions who will not use any form of birth control bringing infected babies into the world and I guess I have lost my social graces. There are a lot of do-gooders out there and it seems I have found some here as well."

"Dr Johnson I am not a do-gooder. I have worked in London at St George's crypt and feel people need me more than sheep and cows. So my farm is for sale since my parents were killed in an accident abroad, and I intend to make some lives a little brighter by bringing them down here for holidays, one day making this place self-sufficient."

"And I am the first lame duck she found and brought me down here when my parents turned me out. I am delighted to have brought the first new life into this venture. I do hope you will come to the opening on August the first, Doctor." Julie was enjoying herself.

"I do not want any preaching at, so I will try my best to avoid this place, and will not be at your beck and call for every little accident," said he looking like thunder.

"Well, Doctor, I think you have an outsized chip on your shoulder, but perhaps with love and patience we will chisel it off."

"It will take more than you to do that." Kate had made him a cup of coffee in the kitchen after which he got into his car laughing, which he hadn't done for a long time. How refreshing to meet someone like Beth. The women he usually met were all trying to attract his attention being so nice to him and he was not interested in any of them. His wife had gone off, with his best friend years ago, since then only work had brought him any consolation. He was not so much against this project as he made out to be, there was something about this Beth that fascinated him. Well, he would not lose any sleep over it or her! He guessed she had a poor little husband doing all the hard work whilst she was 'lady bountiful' in this place.

Later that night Peter, Kate, Beth and Julia were sitting in the lounge when Beth said, "What is the next step in your life, Julie? Do you feel like going to college and what would you study?"

"I have ten O levels and would need to get at least three A levels I would think, but how can I go with the baby to look after? I would like to study Home Economics and nutrition if it was at all possible, but I cannot see how it could be," she said

"Let us ask the Lord what the next step is. If you went to Swansea, Kate and I between us would look after the baby on the days you were away. By the way have you thought of a name for him yet? I cannot wait to get this baby in my arms, Julie, it does not seem likely that I will have children now, so I will be pleased to care for him whilst you are away."

Julie burst out laughing, "You will never guess, I rather like the name Jeremy shortened to Jamie, do you think the doctor would be flattered if I called him that? Or would it make him more conceited than he is already?"

"Well it might well be the start of the chip coming off his shoulder!!" and they all had a good laugh. Kate said she thought the doctor fancied Beth, she saw him laughing as he drove away and he looked so handsome when he smiled.

"I am not looking for a new husband. My past experience in the marriage department is enough for one lifetime."

Chapter 3

Peter and Bill were working on the landscaping around the house and kitchen garden areas. Lots of flowers were purchased from the nursery filling the beds and borders making it look like an old fashioned garden; pinks dahlias, geraniums, all brightly coloured, even some flowering trees. The Budliah attracted so many butterflies and bees - it really looked great. The opening was in two weeks' time and Father Joseph was to bring the first four boys from the east end of London for their holiday. Peter was going to be their carer for the first two weeks showing them the cattle, etc. It was all so exciting. They were all working hard to make the place welcoming.

August the first eventually arrived. All was ready, the extra tables and chairs were in place for the afternoon tea being prepared in the kitchen. Beth went to her room to get changed, out of Jeans into a blue dress with a white collar and shoes. Father Joseph was opening the home officially. Beth was going to outline the activities and aims they hoped to achieve.

"It is our hope that this will be a new beginning for many people. Alpha is the first letter of the Greek alphabet and we hope this home will be the first time many people hear of Jesus and the new life that He can give. We are not going to preach at anyone, that is for sure, hopefully we are going to show them by our love. Jesus said to his disciples before He left them to carry on His work; 'They will know you are Christians by your love one to another', and that is what we hope to follow, although at times it may be difficult. People will come for respite care or a holiday. We shall be a non-profit making organisation, but no one will be turned away because they have no money. We will offer recreational studies, craft, animal husbandry, games; eventually a swimming pool and market garden which we hope will bring in enough cash to oversee the expenses of the project. We hope to supply the village and have a stall on the Swansea market with fresh veg and eggs. I also would like to say any voluntary help in whatever field you are working will be always gratefully accepted. Thank you all for coming today to make this so special. Please wander round have some tea and enjoy the river; it truly is a lovely day. Thank you." Later in the afternoon she saw the doctor gazing into the baby's pram, "Do you know he is called Jeremy, Doctor? He will be known as Jamie."

"Beth I am sorry we got off to a bad start over the delivery of the baby. The people in the village have been telling me about you, you have many admirers there. Out in Africa many people go out to evangelise the natives who are happier, I think, being left alone to their tribal way of life. God does not make new roads and put food in their mouths," he said with feeling.

"Ah, but He does through people. He motivates Christians to go into the world not only to spread the gospel but to build hospitals, dig wells for clean water. So many countries show signs of the British occupation, if that is the right word, when railways were constructed and buildings erected, even I have seen some of this in the places I have been to."

"Well I work mainly in the rural areas and probably see things differently to you, but don't let us fall out again, I am sorry for my rudeness to you, I certainly admire someone who speaks her mind!" When he laughed his face certainly was transformed.

Beth was not sure of this turn of events from being an enemy to a friend … a bit dangerous; she could cope with an enemy, but Jeremy Johnson a friend? Beth was conscious she was looking her best, although she felt more at home in trousers and T-shirt these days. She had long naturally blond hair, too curly for present day fashion, and it was tied back, a very attractive person in Jeremy's eyes.

After the service the guests began to drift away. Beth sat at the kitchen table drinking coffee and eating some of the food left after the tea. She was joined by the rest of the 'team' and eventually Peter and the four new boys. Father Joseph had gone back to London. The boys were a bit subdued by all the people there so after tea Beth took them upstairs with their belongings and settled them into their dormitory. Separate rooms would have been a bit intimidating in a new place. Peter came up to supervise the bathing and hair washing which did not go down too well with them! Beth said a short prayer and told them where her room was in case they wanted her in the night. "It is so dark, Miss, there's no street lights like at home," so for that night they had the single lamp on all night.

Beth went into her downstairs office beside the front door, suddenly she missed her mother. Oh Mum if you were only here with me ... I do miss you so much. Suddenly a hankie was put into her hand and arms went round her hugging her tightly. "Oh Kenneth, I suddenly feel alone, thank you for coming," she put her head on his chest and cried. A minute later she looked up at him to find it was not her cousin but the doctor!

"Do not worry, Beth, I have not seen this vulnerable side of you before, but I am glad that I have. I left my coat here and came to pick it up," he said to himself. He had left it on purpose so that he had to come back!! "You were speaking about showing love to one another. I did not find it hard to put into practice" His mischievous eyes told their own story." Bye now see you again."

"Oh dear I thought you were my cousin Kenneth, I am so sorry." She heard the door close – he had gone, how on earth was she going to handle meeting him next time?

Peter and Julie walked into the village with the four lads. Their names were Michael, James, Josh and Seth. Peter brought them all an ice cream and introduced them to the post mistress. Julie bought stamps for the office. Although the baby was only eight weeks old he had begun to smile and the lads were intrigued with him. On their return Julie suddenly went quiet, she had seen her father's car, a BMW, parked by the house. She picked Jamie out of his pram and went in to face the music. Peter took the boys through the wood to see if they could find the tree house that Beth had told them used to be there.

Julie walked into Beth's sitting room where her mother came with arms outstretched to welcome them both. Father was a bit behind, being uncertain of his welcome, and the reunion Beth had hoped for took place, and they were reconciled. After hugs and tea Julie showed them around. They were thrilled with their first grandchild albeit apprehensive as to the future ... Julie assured them she was staying with Beth and she had arranged for Julie to go to college in Swansea and live at the house. Beth was going to look after Jamie on the days she was away.

"There will be plenty of nurse maids when the girls start coming, Mum, at the moment we are only taking boys."

"How are you financing this establishment, Beth?" asked Julie's father. "We should be financing Julie and are now prepared to do so. She was such a disappointment to us. I'm afraid we did an awful thing turning her out hoping she would learn a lesson from this experience. I happen to know the businessman who has bought your farm, he is a client of mine he told me your story, then your letter came telling us that Julie was here. He is very impressed and we would like to help by setting up sponsorship. He obviously has been to your old home, although his manager is living there now, he would like to come down here and see you next time he visits." Julie was very thrilled that her father said this and that Beth had brought this reconciliation about.

Beth told them the story and said she had enough money to carry on for a long time yet but obviously soon the Home would be self-financing. "It is a Christian Home, Mr Cartwright, and we trust the Lord to show us the way He wants the Home to run. Some people coming for holidays will pay a small contribution, those coming to help will be free. I have lost my parents and my husband who wants to be free to travel the world and is not likely to return so I can do something to help others. Cows and sheep do not need me, people do." She smiled as she shook the outstretched hand as if sealing a contract.

Chapter 4

Every night when the boys were in bed Beth told them a Bible story relating to what they had been doing on that day. "

"Have you had a good day boys?"

"Yes, Miss, we have, and we found that tree house and Mr Peter is going to help us mend it so we can have our meals up there, he told us you had tents as well and we can sleep in the woods. Cor, Miss, I never knew there's such places like this." Josh was excited

"Have you seen the animals yet? The sheep and cows, hens and ducks?" asked Beth.

"No that is for tomorrow, if we have time after the tree house," said Michael.

"Do you know what Christmas is all about?"

"Yes, Miss, presents if you're lucky and the money goes round," this was Seth speaking.

"We do have a bit more to eat on that day," said James, and that seemed to go for all of them.

"No I mean the real reason we have Christmas? It is to celebrate the birth of Jesus as a baby; He was born in a stable in Bethlehem because they could not find a room in the inn. Then when He was only small they had to go a long way on a donkey into Egypt because Herod the king wanted to kill Him. Jesus was born to be King not of an earthly kingdom but a Christian kingdom. Have you heard of this story before?" they did not seem to know, "Well we will go on another night about what happened to Him. OK now snuggle down and no messing about I am just around the corridor from here so I can hear you. Come to me if you need me in the night. I will leave alight on. Good night, boys, God bless you."

This was the best part of the day. Julie and Kate with Peter nursing Jamie were waiting for her to come in. "Hot chocolate, Beth, we have had a wonderful day, let us really thank God for what has happened," Kate said.

"Well thank you, Lord, for bringing reconciliation for Julie and Jamie today, only you could have softened their hearts and made them sorry for what they did to Julie. Thank you for bringing her here with our darling Jamie, may they both come to know you as their Saviour and Peter, too. We thank you for Julie's father and the sponsorship idea it, is beyond belief what You will do if we trust You to do things which we feel are impossible. Bless these dear boys, keep them safe, show us what things you want us to do with them This is for your glory Lord not ours, Amen. We will have a staff meeting tomorrow to see how many more staff we need at the moment, plans for the market garden and bringing the cows and sheep down from the farm which I kept before the sale." said Beth.

On the whole the first fortnight had gone very well. Only one fight between James and Seth over seconds at dinner time one day! Michael took himself into the wood and got lost so that night they had the story of the lost sheep when the shepherd went out to find the one which was lost. Michael said he was very frightened in the wood alone, he was so glad when Peter came to find him. They all took to their new diet after the second day. Good wholesome food not chips with everything, they loved Kate's puddings. They were now ready to go back to London reluctantly.

"Well,"said Beth, "If you did not go home you could never come again."

"When can we come again, Miss?"

"We will make a list of all who have been and next year we might have room for you," she was so glad that they had enjoyed the time with them.

At two o'clock Peter had them down at the station ready to meet Father Joseph who was bringing the next four down and returning with the others. A bright young man jumped out of the train introducing himself as the new curate. Jason Fairbrother.

"I am new to the job but this is the easy part of it, these kids have never seen the countryside before, I don't know how you are going to get on with them here, by the way do you need an extra pair of hands, my contract does not start until October, I could do five weeks if you need me? I could come down on the train."

"They have been praying for another pair of hands, I can't understand how this God works. They seem to pray for things and then they happen." Peter said to Jason. He could not understand how some of this prayer stuff worked.

"That would be great, working in London's East end is going to be tough for a Yorkshire lad, but I am determined to give it a go." Meanwhile the old lads were frightening the new ones to death about getting lost maybe falling in the river!!

"Do not take any notice of them, these things will not happen if you keep the rules of the home. Come on now I guess you are hungry after such an early start I know we have meat pie waiting for us and apple crumble."

"What is crumble mister?"

"Just you wait and see. My name is Peter and you may call me that."

Very quickly they arrived at the home. Beth was outside to meet them.

"Hello, boys, welcome to Alpha Home, we are glad that you are here and hope you are going to enjoy yourselves. The meal is ready so leave your bags in the hall and follow me."

They all sat round the kitchen table Peter, Julie, Bill came in and Beth. Kate served the meal which was enjoyed by them all, the boys had second helpings! After tea Beth spelt out the rules of the home, not many, but necessary for its smooth running.

"You all need to have a bath and hair wash tonight and when you are in bed a story time."

"We don't want a bath and a story, we are not kids, Miss," Jacko obviously was the spokesman.

"A bath is compulsory but you need not listen to the story, I know you are all eleven but I still like a story even at my great age."

"What's compulsory, Miss?"

Beth thought for a minute, "It means you have to do it. It is better to do what you are told, that makes for a happier time for everyone." said Beth.

Jacko was one to be watched and handled carefully – a ring leader. They were so tired the story time was missed after they all were bathed and hair washed with special shampoo!! Beth said good night, told them where her room was if they needed her during the night.

On Sundays all the staff and children were encouraged to go to the village Church in the morning. If the children did not want to go Peter would stay behind and show them round the farm. The children decided to 'give it a go' so they all piled into two cars and reached the church in time. The vicar was very pleased to see them and welcomed them; they really enjoyed being celebrities. The people were very friendly as well and they were invited to play football on Tuesday with the youth club. To Beth's surprise Dr Jeremy was sitting in the back pew. After the service he waited for her going out.

"I only came to church to see you, Beth, could I take you out for a meal one night? I guess you could do with a change of scene and company." He seemed quite nervous, a change for him!

"Well that is a kind thought, but I do tell the lads a Bible story when they are in bed, then it is quite late. Would you come to the home for a meal? We can have it in my private sitting room or I could get one of the others to tell the story for me. Where had you in mind? She was so surprised. "Give me a ring when you have sorted something out or tell me what and where. I will have to go now I am doing dinner today, it is easy; soup, salad, cold meat, etc., with hot high tea at 6.00p.m. to follow, you may join us if you can stand the noise!"

"Thanks but I am on call today; will ring you later tonight. Bye now." With that he went hurrying down the road to his house.

Life is full of surprises thought Beth as she started her car, what will Kate say to this dinner date, he must be very lonely to invite me out! She had mixed feelings he was so attractive but she did not want to get involved with anyone else, "Goodness, girl." she said to herself, "It is only a dinner, not a proposal!"

That night when the children were in bed Julie joined them with Jamie. She sat on John's bed and listened to the story. "Did you see any sheep today in the field boys? Well our story is about a shepherd, the man who looks after the sheep. Not Mr Bill, but in the Bible days they had a sheepfold, that is the place where the sheep sleep at night. Can you imagine a square piece of land with walls on four sides but a small opening on one side where the sheep go in? I have drawn a picture for you. The shepherd stands at the opening counting the sheep as they go in to rest for the night, he knows how many there should be and if there is one missing he blocks up the door way and goes out looking for the one who is lost because he loves his sheep very much. It might take him all night and he is tired as well, but he keeps on searching until he can take the sheep back to the pen. Why do you think the sheep got lost? Perhaps it was naughty and thought the grass was better in another field, or perhaps he fell down a hole because he was curious and wanted to know what was at the bottom, but whatever the reason he needed to be found. Do you know, boys, we are like those sheep; we do wrong things and hope we do not get found out. Sometimes we think we know better than our teachers and parents and get into trouble with the police or make other people sad. How many of us wish we could be kinder and more loving to others? Well Jesus is the good shepherd and if we ask Him to help us in our lives and confess the things we have done wrong He will make us His children or sheep and keep us safe. We might not ask Him until we get into trouble but He always hears our prayers. We are going to talk to him now. Dear Lord Jesus, thank you for wanting me in your family, please help me to want to come to you and ask you into my life for your dear sake. Amen." Two boys were already asleep. Beth kissed them all and left the small light on. You know where my room is if you need me in the night.

"Will your door be open; because my mam says if her door is shut she has a man with her and we don't go in I would not like that to happen to you? She says if she had not got a man with her we would not have any food to eat." Jacko – always the spokesman.

"I do not have a man in my room ever so I am there for you all. Good night, boys. God bless."

Oh dear what some poor folks have to put up with, dear Lord, is there no other way?

Julie followed Beth into her sitting room. "I am a lost sheep, Beth, not wanting to come into His family. For a long time I have rejected Him and made excuses for my sin, but tonight I want to put that right, to confess and be forgiven, to become His child."

Beth was overjoyed and prayed for her that she would find peace. "Beth, one of the things which I cannot get over is the fact that you took me in knowing what I was like and pregnant; you accepted me, loved me, and never preached at me, that to me has been so wonderful."

"Julie, we have all sinned in one way or another and God takes us as we are, warts and all, we cannot hide anything

58

from him. He knows us and loves us, just tell Him now and I will pray for you."

Beth was so thrilled that this had happened. Although it was late she had to tell somebody so she rang Father Joseph with the good news.

After breakfast Jacko talked to Beth; as she was washing up she gave him a tea towel. "You were talking about the shepherd looking for the sheep, my mum would not go looking for me, when I was coming here she said if I did not come back it did not matter it would be one less mouth to feed. I have six brothers and two sisters and there is not enough food to go round often, so I go round Tesco's bins and there is lovely food that is supposed to be old but it tastes good, so I take some home if there is a lot. My dad drinks a lot, comes home drunk, so we get out of the way upstairs."

"Well, Jacko your mum must have a hard time looking after all your family, don't think too badly of her, I am sure she does her best. You can take some treats for them when you go home." Beth replied.

After dinner the boys sat round the table and a list of things they could do was read out. Things like roaming in the wood, seeing the cattle and farm, collecting eggs for the market, learning basic cooking, reading, playing football, collecting wood for the fires for the winter months, or helping Peter to work in the market garden he was making. They made a list of what they wanted to do for the week, although it was altered when they found something they really enjoyed doing. That afternoon they decided to go for a walk around the farm, beside the river and up into the woods. They began their walk by the new swimming pool which was almost finished.

"I think before you go home you will be able to have a swim in here, we have got trunks for boys and goggles, and also floats so that you don't sink. Peter will teach you to swim but you must not come in here alone, you must always be with a member of staff in case of accidents." Beth was careful to warn them of the dangers,

"What's goggles, Miss?" asked John.

"They are fings which go over your eyes," said Jacko.

"Well how can you see if they are over your eyes?" asked John.

"They are like glasses only bigger, you daft dope." Jacko was top dog at the moment.

"Now then you two, we won't have any name calling. If there is anything you want to know just do not be afraid to ask." Beth led them to the cows and explained that the cows gave us milk; she called Peter to demonstrate milking a cow. The children stood in awe, "I do not want any of that stuff coming out of those things, Miss. I get it out of the supermarket in containers, it is better than that." Jacko was disgusted.

"Where do you think the supermarkets get their milk from?" Peter and Beth could hardly contain their laughter. "Did you have cornflakes for breakfast with milk on them?" she asked. "The milk is taken to the dairy and cooled then refrigerated. Come I will show you and then we will all have a glass of lovely milk given by the cow this morning."

"Mr Peter, where did you learn to do that, pulling those things?" Jacko again the spokesman,

"I have spent three yours in college learning," he was amused by their questions.

"Gosh it must be hard if it took you that long, did you learn to do other things as well?"

"Yes I can sheer a sheep, deliver a calf, help the sheep when they are having lambs, as well as drive a tractor and lots more besides," he replied.

"A walk through the woods now, boys, no more biology lessons today." She thought the tree house was safer ground.

John said, "My mam said keep away from animals or they trample on yer in the country. So I shall not go near them, hens peck as well."

"Ours will not do that unless you frighten them or make them run."

Beth thought the woods were less of a problem than explaining about sheep giving wool and milk and hens laying eggs; enough for today she felt.

"Would you like to sleep out in the woods one night? We have got tents and I am sure Mr Jason would sleep there with you. I used to sleep out here when I was your age with my friends; it is good fun to wake up in the morning with the river running by and making tea on a little stove." They were not sure about that but did mention it to Jason at supper time. He agreed to put up the tent the next day to get them used to it.

The bungalow for Kate was almost finished. She had been so excited to choose carpets, bathroom and kitchen furniture. Bill was at The Alpha Home full time now caring for the animals overseeing the egg production whilst Peter was sharing looking after the children with Jason, on other days he set up the market garden. There were only kidney beans at the moment for sale but plastic tunnels would encourage seeds to grow for next year.

The Vicar rang the next morning to ask if they had a vacancy for a part-time office girl. His wife wanted a little job other than being the vicar's wife! Beth was delighted and arranged to see her later on that day. This was good news. There is a text that says 'Before they call I will answer'. They met over a cup of tea settled the salary and Rebecca began work the next morning. Another phone call was from the doctor with a date for the following night for dinner at a village pub in Bryn Dower a few miles away. Fortunately she found she was looking forward to this event, and immediately wondered what she would wear, she had nice clothes that did not see the light of day in her present life, perhaps one of them could have an airing!

Things were ticking over quite well; Beth felt quite relaxed as she got ready for the dinner date. Peter and Julie were telling the story of the feeding of the five thousand that evening. Jeremy picked her up at 6.30p.m.; their meal was booked for 8p.m., there had been a lot of leg pulling at lunchtime when the rest of them found out about the 'date'. We are a family, Beth thought amid all the banter, although it was at her expense. There was a lovely view over the mountains, Jeremy stopped the car and they walked for a little way over a grassy field. Beth was wearing a light pink dress, high-heeled shoes which were not good on grass, and a pink bag. The meal was very good homemade food, which was what Beth ate each day, but it was a treat for Jeremy. He asked how the home was coming on being very amused at some of the stories she was recalling especially about the bed room door being open or shut! "Tell me about your work in Africa."

"After a very sad time when my wife went off with my best friend I felt cross and let down. She had deceived me as well, I volunteered for the research programme in Africa which lasted for five years this is my fourth year; I go back in May for one more year then maybe get a practice around here if possible. I have enjoyed Wales, this part especially. You must have thought me a real horror when you rang me about that first delivery, I am sorry I was such a horror, I was doing my thesis on my findings and it was at a critical part. I got totally the wrong picture of you being like a hospital matron! However when I saw you I felt ashamed and too proud to say sorry. I should not listen to gossip, I know, but I did hear you have been married?" said Jeremy.

"Yes a marriage of convenience," then she told him the whole story about her parents being killed, the village gossips, and how God spoke to her about setting up the Alpha Home."

"I am very interested, Beth, I do wish I had your faith. I felt it was all God's fault when I was so unhappy. Then going to Africa I must confess I met missionaries who were not like you, but doing it for their own ego, were not practical Christians and criticised my work because I was advocating birth control; it sickened me to see babies born with AIDS and babies dying, or Mothers dying leaving little children often with an uncaring father or none at all. Sorry, Beth, I should not get steamed up about it. You, my dear Beth, would be torn to bits over there; your compassion would boil over and frustrate you because we are only scratching the surface. How can I believe in a God who lets this happen?" said Jeremy with conviction.

"Free will, Jeremy, God has given us all a free will to do as we please that is the only way I came to terms with my parents' deaths. The driver had been drinking I believe and his choice had caused many people suffering; he used his free will to hurt others. I often wonder how many I have hurt by making the wrong choices, not killing them physically, but unintentionally killing friendships, relationships, etc., it is a sobering thought, but it is not going to spoil our evening, come on let us go for a walk around this pretty little village now we have had dinner."

When Jeremy dropped her off much later he came in for a coffee. She then took him to the door where he lingered, Beth I have enjoyed being with you; do you mind a good night kiss?" Actually, although she would not admit it to herself … she was longing for it!

The boys' fortnight came to an end. They had loved being out of doors and the weather had been very good. The next lot were due on Saturday and it all had to be repeated.

Chapter 5

It was interesting to see the different reactions they had to the activities. Jason bid a fond goodbye to us all to take up his duties with Father Joseph in London in September. The nights were getting darker and the weather cooler. The activities changed from outdoor to indoor games in the evenings after tea. However, outside walks and the swimming continued. Beth was concerned with herself. She thought so much about Jeremy the doctor and was so afraid she was falling in love with him. The kiss, fleeting though it might have been, awakened feelings she had denied herself for so long. Also by now she thought they might have had some adults coming for a rest or retreat. The other good thing that had happened, Julie's father had bought her a car to go to college in Swansea every day. That was wonderful. One day this car arrived with a card tied to the door handle. 'With our love and good wishes for your course, Mum and Dad'. Peter taught her how to drive very quickly, after which she passed her test. It was handy Julie going into Swansea, she took over the shopping, leaving Beth free to look after Jamie.

In October four boys came who were so much more boisterous, they had been before. These really were street types. They had heard about The Alpha Home and been to ask Father Joseph if they could come. He was dubious, but Jason said they would be welcome – little did he know!

Beth and the team welcomed them on arrival; one lad was almost in the river before they had been introduced. "Come in, boys, and have some tea and a chat about the home and what we expect of you and you of us."

"We know all about this place, Miss, the other lads told us, I am Pete this is Shawn the sheep, Bill and Sam. We are all in the same gang at home and we hang out together." Obviously the leader!

"Good," said Beth. "Now we will introduce ourselves. I am Beth, the boss of the home, these are also bosses. That is Mr Peter he deals with the market garden, Mr Bill who is the farmer, Mrs Kate who, with Julie's help, is the cook, so keep on the right side of her! Rebecca is in the office, Jason has had to go back to London to be the curate of St Georges Church, we are looking for a replacement for him. Oh and this is Jamie, our latest recruit. We do not have a lot of rules, but no swearing, smoking or name calling either of mates or staff. If you want anything ask us and we will try to get it for you. If you want to go to the village it is a mile down the road and within easy walking distance, but you must ask one of us to go with you. OK? Now bring your things upstairs, unpack and dinner is at 6.30.p.m." When they had gone she said to the others, "We have got to keep a step ahead of these boys."

The first night went fairly well after they had realised the bath and hair wash was essential. No story the first night. They did not go to Church on Sunday neither did Peter who stayed with them. Monday morning after breakfast Beth took Jamie and gave them a tour of inspection.

The first stop was the hens in a shed on wheels with a large enclosure of wire to keep the foxes out; this could be moved to different places in the orchard. She showed them where the nesting boxes were, "One job for you is to collect the eggs every day and not to break any because they have to be washed before being sold."

"How do they lay eggs, Miss, where do they come from?" asked Bill.

"Miss, they come from its backside, I seed it in a book!" said Sam.

"They come down the birth canal from the uterus as if they were giving birth to the chicks, only the chicks will not hatch because we eat the yolks when we cook them. Next we have the cows up in the top field, perhaps Bill will come with us as he knows more about cows than I do."

"What's those things hanging near their back legs, Miss?" Sam was curious this time.

"They are called udders, they are really milk bags holding the milk until they go to be milked either by machine or hand. We can take you up to the farm and see them milking one day."

"I don't like all this I like supermarket milk, not coming out of those things," Shawn was not happy about the milk supply. All the children found milk a problem.

"Where do you think the supermarket gets the milk from? How strange you all say that but you have to know these things you are growing up." Beth then took them to the sheep field, this must be better. "What do we get from sheep?"

They looked a bit mystified, "Meat, although I aint had any. My mam says its costs too much to have meat," said little Sam.

"We get wool from the wool on their backs; every summer they have their hair cut, they are shorn and the wool is sold and made into clothes and blankets. Sheep's wool is very warm; I will show you a sheep skin back at the house. The wool grows again before the winter comes because when they are in the field and when it is snowing they need to keep warm." Beth had left their sheep dogs up at the farm because there was not enough work for them here and they were working dogs. "I must get another dog, it is not good to be without one," she thought to herself.

"All ready for tea? I am, come on let's see what Kate has made for us today." Julie was in the kitchen preparing the tea.

"Can we have a paddle in the river, Miss?" Asked Sam, all this talk of eggs, cow's milk, sheep and wool had thoroughly confused him, paddling in water he did understand, he was a slow learner. "I fort we had come for a holiday, Miss, this is like school I want to enjoy myself."

"And so you shall, Sam, but we thought as you don't have these animals in London you would like to know all about them and perhaps help Mr Bill and Peter to look after them, perhaps collect the eggs for us?"

"No, Miss, I aint touching them, any of them, them cows look vicious to me," did Sam speak for them all, Beth wondered, if so they would do other things with them the first week, it was hard to know what they are thinking, this was a totally different environment to what they were used.

"Bed time. Have a good wash or shower, I will come in when you are in bed."

"You are a bit fussy, Miss. My mam lets us go straight to bed when we have been playing, we don't wash as much as we do here. What is the story tonight, Miss?" strange how they all liked the story time after the first night when they thought they were too old for stories …

"The story tonight is about creation. That means how the world began. The Bible tells us that God made the world in seven days that seems a short time to make all the living things on the earth. Adam and Eve, his wife, were the first people living in a lovely garden called Eden. God said they could eat any fruit and the things that grew in the garden, but one thing they could not eat were the apples of the tree in the middle of the garden. Life must have been great there, sunny weather, beautiful flowers, all the animals loving each other. Until one day Eve was sitting near the special tree when a snake came up to her and told her to eat the apples from the forbidden tree. "If you eat them they will make you as wise as God. When Adam came to her she told him and gave him one to eat. That evening as it was getting dark, God walked in the garden. Usually they enjoyed talking to God but this night they tried to avoid Him. Then He called out "Adam where are you?" then Adam knew had been disobedient in eating the apples which God had forbidden him to do. Then God said they were going to be turned out of the garden into the world outside where he had to work hard to become a farmer, to look after the animals, make vegetables grow and do all the things which we have to do now to live. Whilst Adam obeyed God he was free do what he liked, all his needs were supplied. God called disobedience a sin, and like a lot of sins we do not get away with them unless we ask God to forgive us, He will do that if we are truly sorry.

Some people think there is no God, but who started the world, no-one has come up with a better story. We don't know how long was seven days, it might have been seven years. Some rocks are thousands of years old that was before this story happened." As Beth looked up they were sleepy. No one asked any questions, she gave them a good night kiss and tucked them in.

Beth flopped down on her settee and kicked off her shoes!! It had been a long day. A knock at the door; Jeremy came in with a tray of coffee and biscuits which Julie had given him to take up to Beth.

"Oh do come in Jeremy you are most welcome bringing refreshments, I feel really tired tonight. It is good to see you." Beth felt so pleased that he had called uninvited. He asked what she had been doing with the children that day and they were amused at some of their reaction to the cattle, especially the milk problem. Kate was going to put some in a container so they would think it was from the supermarket. It was quite late when Jeremy went home. Beth went to the front door with him, and was quite pleased when he kissed her briefly good night. The chemistry seems to be there she thought!! Oh Lord I do not want to make another mistake!

Chapter 6

Beth was thinking it was time to build the Quiet Room" in remembrance of her parents Not to be called a church, that might put some people off using it. After breakfast she rang Zachary Pemberton to ask if he would come out and measure up. He made an appointment for the next day to stay to lunch as well. It was to be a room holding about 50 people with comfortable chairs for them to relax and meditate or read quietly. Along the back wall book shelves containing all kinds of books, Christian and secular story books and novels. Also there had to be a small room like a vestry for coat hanging, a small kitchen to make tea and toilet facilities, with a plaque inside the front door with her parents name. Also whilst Zachary was there he could create plans for a conservatory to the front of the home overlooking the river. Beth envisaged tables and chairs for afternoon teas for people from the village, hikers or anyone needing a cup of tea. This became so popular that eventually they had to have a log cabin as well.

After lunch the next day Zachary asked Beth if she had the time to walk through the woods with him. He wanted to find out what motivated her to spend her money in this way. He was very impressed by what he had seen, the boys at lunch intrigued him, totally uninhibited they had talked about their homes and the unusual way of life that was normal for them in London.

"There must be something that keeps you motivated to do this work, Beth, I am curious to know what it is?" he said as they walked by the river.

"My motivation comes from being a Christian, feeling the need to help those less fortunate than myself. I worked in the crypt on my days off from the hospital, in the evenings we took soup and bread out, got involved with some of the homeless, even getting some back into their homes again. I want to develop The Alpha Home truly into a home of new beginnings for some people not only children for holidays. Who knows, in the future we might have a nursing home attached, then we will be asking you for plans for that!"

They got back in time for tea. Julie had been to the village to take Jamie for his injections. Jeremy was asking for you, Beth, he is concerned that you might be doing too much, I assured him that we are all here keeping an eye on you. I got the feeling that he also intends to do that, you have made a hit there, Beth; I somehow think we are going to see much more of Dr Jeremy here."

Julie was right! Several days later it was Beth's turn to take the boys rambling. They assembled outside the front door kitted up for walking, having made their own sandwiches, now in their back packs, when down the Lane came another hiker. "Good morning, Beth, I see I am too late to take you walking that was my intention," Dr Jeremy sounded none too pleased.

"Ah do join us, Doctor, we would love to have your company, we have enough lunch packed to feed an army and I know of a lovely spot to eat it."

"Well that is not what I had in mind but seeing that it is your duty day I will go along with you. Come on, chaps, are you good walkers?" he said.

"We don't go in woods very often at home if we climb trees and fall out of them, it will be good to have our own doctor with us." Sam had taken a liking to the doctor and walked closely by his side. The boys frequently asked if they were there yet and was it dinner time? It was with some relief they found the spot where Beth's father had put a picnic table by the river, where they had shared many happy times. She tried not to be emotional when she told them, but Jeremy saw her bright eyes and feeling sorry for her he said, "Come on then where is this food, I am starving?"

Whilst they were eating Beth asked him to tell them about Africa, the poor children who were very much worse off than they were in England, who were suffering from AIDS. These kids were street kids they had heard of AIDS, even knowing people who had AIDS on their street; they also knew how they had got it.

"We have been warned not to go with prostitutes, Miss, cos if they have it they can pass it on to the fellows." These were eleven year olds.

"Goodness you are not old enough to know anything about prostitutes." Beth was quite surprised, at the turn the conversation had taken

"I know, Miss, because my mam is one," Shawn said. "But I don't think she has AIDS or she would have told us, I have six brothers and sisters she needs the money. She does love us, Miss, that's why she does it. She looks lovely when she goes out, not on the streets, but to his house … my dad does not mind her doing that as long as she gives him some money for the pub."

"Why am I going to Africa to research when I could stay in London and do research here?" wondered Jeremy. He was quite surprised at this conversation but the children carried on about other people they knew who were in the same occupation. Beth then started to tell them about loving marriage and keeping themselves clean for the person they were going to fall in love with one day.

"Are you two getting married then?" asked Bill who had been very quiet throughout the conversation, being brought up by his grandmother, having no idea where his mother was. "It must be lovely to have a mother and father," he added, wistfully.

"I think we will be married one day," said Jeremy. "But don't tell her because I have not asked her yet," he had such a mischievous look in his eyes. Beth was blushing saying it is time to go home!

"Don't leave it too long because she is a lovely lady and someone else might get her," said Sam, the ever practical one.

It was a very merry party that walked home, they marched and sang 'When the saints go marching in', and 'Ten green bottles hanging on the wall'. It was almost dark when they reached the Home. They said good bye to Jeremy as he was walking on to the village. "Are you going to kiss her then seeing that you are going to marry her?" Pete called out, cheekily, and with lots of laughter they obliged!

"What is the story tonight, Miss"?

"I think it has to be the marriage at Cana in Galilee. When Jesus and his Mother were there the wine ran out, and they had not enough to drink. So Jesus told them to fill the water pots full of water and then pour it out to the bride groom. He asked them why they had left the best wine until the last, usually they serve the best wine first and the greedy ones then had the worst watered down stuff. Jesus performed the first miracle, he did many more afterwards. Jesus is with us all through our lives and He wants to work miracles in our lives if we will ask Him to help us to do the right things. If you want to know more about the Christian life I will answer your questions. By the way you did put us in a spot this dinner time, the doctor and I hardly know each other, we are only friends." With that she kissed them good night. 'Out of the mouths of babes!... But these were hardly babes going by the conversation at dinner time!

Two things happened which caused Beth some concern. Nellie Green the post mistress rang her to say that two boys had been in the shop, one bought some sweets. After they had gone she found four bars of chocolate were missing and some crisps. She had never had any problems with the boys before or girls either. They were not supposed to go to the village alone. Could Beth investigate when they arrived home please? Beth assured her the boys would be brought back to pay for them.

Pete and Sam looked a bit sheepish. "Come here boys and empty your pockets please." There were two bars left and crisps. "Where are the rest of the chocolate bars, have you eaten them on the way home? I am afraid we have got to go back and pay for them and apologise to the post mistress for stealing them. Which one of you did it?"

"We were both in it, Miss, we decided to do it together. Please, Miss, I do this all the time at home, my Dad showed me how not to get court. And it is easy in the supermarkets because the shelves are high and they can't see what you are doing; if you have a big coat on with pockets it is easy."

"Come on get in the car we have to go to say sorry otherwise she will call the local policeman, and that has never happened before. You do have spending money get that ready to pay for them." said Beth sadly.

Pete was very upset, he had been taught to steal and pick pockets so he didn't really know what all the fuss was about. Nellie was very vocal in her torrent of accusations. A very subdued Pete paid for what he owed and apologised profusely. Beth sent them out of the shop and told Nellie how Pete's father had taught him to steal, but Beth would have a word later on with them. It was difficult when parents taught different values to their children; she did not want to alienate them from their families.

That night they had the story of Zacchaeus the tax collector who had stolen people's money, charging them more than he should and keeping much of it for himself. She told how he had heard of Jesus and when He came down the road with a crowd of people following Him, Zacchaeus climbed into a tree and hide in the branches so that Jesus would not see him. When Jesus came under the tree He looked up and saw Zacchaeus. He looked up and said "Come down, Zacchaeus for today I am coming to your house for tea." Fancy Jesus coming to his house when he was a thief. All the people hated him because he stole their money. When Jesus talked to him he then said how sorry he was and asked God to forgive him, he then said he would give the people back the money he had taken from them and give them more besides. He was pleased Jesus had forgiven him; he then became a follower of Jesus telling others that God would forgive their sins if they said they were truly sorry and turned away from the life of sin they had been living. "Jesus can do that for us today if we ask him to." Beth did not want to teach against what his father had taught him but it was only a matter of time before the police would find out what they had stolen.

Beth decided it was time for some of the girls to have a chance to come for a holiday. It was coming up to Christmas and the weather was getting colder. She had a store cupboard of clothes and shoes, wellingtons and boots, woolly jumpers, hats and scarves for the walks in the woods, as well as collecting the eggs and feeding the fowls. Father Joseph contacted the social workers and four little girls came down in November. They loved the kitchen, Julie taught them some basic cooking, stews, apple pies, cakes; things they would be able to do at home hopefully!

Mary Jane was one small girl for her twelve years very withdrawn hardly speaking and eating very little. Beth called Jeremy to have a chat with her about the child and they felt she had some problem which was holding her back. The third night after the story and good night kiss Beth thought she heard crying in the girls' room. Mary Jane was sobbing, the others were asleep so Beth took her to her sitting room and gave her a cuddle. For a long time she would not tell Beth why she was crying, then eventually she said it was because her father was coming out of prison at Christmas time." Before he went into prison he said he would kill my mother and me when he got out, and we have nowhere to go, we are afraid he will come to our house and get us, Miss."

"Why did he go to prison?" "Because he used to do bad things to me and my friends when my mother was out working cleaning offices in the evening. She didn't really believe me when I told her but my friend went to the police station. They came and took him away and he thinks I told them. I did not do that to him. We only visited him once in prison and he said he would kill us."

"Have you got relatives to go to?"

"No, my mother has no one, they did not want her to marry him so had nothing to do with us, I don't even know my grandparents," she said, sadly.

"Look we will sort something out, Mary Jane, and if there is nowhere else, you can both come here and stay with us. If she would like to your mother could work here and you could go to the local school. I will ring Father Joseph. I am sure he will have a solution. Let me pray with you now. And ask God to work something out for you both. Go to sleep now it will be better in the morning."

As usual Beth flopped down on her lounge chair feeling tired and worried – the things these children had to put up with, she felt very sad for them. The phone rang then, wearily she answered.

"Beth, its Jeremy, can you possibly come and help me, the local midwife is on another case and I have a difficult birth, there is not time to take her to Swansea; it is 20 Newlands Street. See you," and with that he put the phone down,

Beth found Peter and Julie playing with Jamie in the lounge downstairs. She explained where she was going; they could lock up she would take the key, quickly she told them about Mary Jane's problem.

Driving down to Newlands Street her mind was in a turmoil, prisons, murders new births. "Please Lord help me to concentrate on the baby and Jeremy. Help us please to make this a safe delivery, a live baby and save the mother."

On entering the living room, Jeremy said; "Beth, this is May. Together we must deliver her baby." May's mother was looking so worried.

"Thank goodness you have come to help the doctor," Jeremy barely looked at her as she entered the room. "I may have to do a caesarean section, Beth, the baby is the wrong way , I cannot move it at all," the perspiration was dripping from his forehead and Beth wiped it as she had done many times in theatre during operations. May was almost unconscious, Beth spoke to her gently,

"I am going to pray now, May."

With that she laid her hands on the baby and beseeched the Lord to turn this child so that it could be born naturally. Within a few minutes her hands felt an eruption in the uterus and the bay had turned causing some pain but was now ready to be born. Beth looked at Jeremy and smiled, "Better now." He certainly looked more relieved. Within 20 minutes the baby was born. Although the baby was alive she needed an incubator and oxygen. The ambulance came without an incubator so Beth wrapped her up warmly and snuggled her close to her chest. The baby had an oxygen mask on. Both Mother and baby survived. They handed them over to the hospital staff who were waiting for them, had a cup of coffee and took a taxi home.

"Have you ever heard of anyone being jealous of a baby, Beth"? asked Jeremy sitting in the back seat holding her hand. "Because I was when I saw that baby snuggled up to your bosom and wished it was me." He suddenly felt relaxed; he had never felt so inadequate in all his life, if the baby had not turned he would not have had the equipment to do caesarean section and there would not have been time to go to Swansea before the baby was in real trouble, he could have lost them both. It was a miracle.

"Well," said Beth, "you will have to be satisfied with holding my hand, you are too big for anything else now," she laughed from relief that it was all over. Beth then told him about Mary Jane's problem.

"If her Mother wants to come then she can do so, we have plenty of rooms, I am in touch with Father Joseph, I rang him last night."

"You do need protection. Does Peter sleep on your corridor? I know you have God, you proved that tonight, but a man about the home would be good." Jeremy came into the kitchen with her, the rest of them were having breakfast.

"Have you two spent the night together?" The little cheeky monkey said, grinning. "Yes as a matter of fact we have, delivering a baby and taking it with the mother to Swansea hospital, where hopefully they are both going to be alright." She then told them of the miracle that God had done in turning the baby when she prayed." We will both have bacon and eggs I think Julie and then its bed for me, so, Peter, can you cope with these four today, please? I will get up at dinner time. Have you got a surgery this morning, Jeremy? I hope not."

Chapter 7

Beth was thinking of Christmas as she walked to church on Sunday morning, it was quite cold and the girls this week had decided to stay at home. After the service she spoke to the vicar and Rebecca his wife about the arrangements for a party at The Alpha Home perhaps on Christmas Eve.

"A general invitation for all the village people with a short thanksgiving service for the months the home has been open. The quiet room should be ready then so we can use that and have the food in the dining room with extra tables and chairs. Perhaps a barn dance if we can get some musicians. I want it to be a very happy time."

"I heard about you helping with the delivery the other night and the dash with Dr Jeremy to Swansea, also I heard that you prayed over the baby and it turned, so that it could be born normally," the vicar was so glad when he heard this.

"We give God all the glory for that, it truly was a miracle. Jeremy was really stressed about it, I hope he acknowledges that God did the miracle; I am praying for another miracle that he will become a Christian. At the moment he shows no signs of it! But miracles do happen."

The week before Christmas was very busy. Invitations had been sent out to uncle and cousin John and Kenneth and his wife, in Scotland and to Julie's mother and father in London. Mary Jane and her Mother were already staying at the home, they had literally walked out of their house with their belongings before the husband had come out of prison, so that he had some where to stay .They did not want him to find them but had to wait to see what the future held for them. They shared a room being very comfortable and were a really big help in the house, they worked hard not minding what they were asked to do.

Peter brought in a large Christmas tree from the woods. There was a lot of fun decorating it. Beth had taken Julie shopping in Swansea to buy presents for everybody, small things for the villagers much larger ones for the household staff. Several turkeys had been resident at the farm, these were for the dinner although they were careful not to tell the children this! Julie had two friends at the collage who unfortunately could not go home for Christmas so they came to help in the kitchen. Jamie was now six months old and a real treasure, Beth loved him dearly spending a lot of time with him whilst going for walks with the children and playing games. Peter also was devoted to him, often putting him to bed and feeding him. The quiet room was ready several days before Christmas. The walls were painted a very light shade of yellow, with a blue carpet and blue and golden coloured upholstered chairs. There was a plain oak table at the front with a small modern piano to the left wall. The heaters made a lovely warm atmosphere and a real sense of peace. A large beautiful silk flower arrangement of Christmas flowers was on the table also one in the small porch by the door. For this time a Christmas tree stood by the table nicely decorated with presents beneath it. Beth was alone in the quiet place before locking it up; she thanked God for every remembrance of her parents without whose money she could not have brought happiness to many lives already.

Christmas Eve and six o'clock; Beth had been busy all day preparing food and the dining room for the party, the tables were literally groaning with it! The house looked bright with shining garlands, holly and mistletoe, flowers and bowls of fruit and nuts. The house guests were down first having a cup of tea before the thanksgiving in the quiet room which filled up very quickly after six. Beth played a few carols which everyone enjoyed singing and then the vicar stood up to talk about Beth's parents and the farm they enjoyed; how they helped the village and how delighted they would be that Beth had made the Alpha Home. A place of new beginnings. He dedicated it then in prayer. It was not a sad occasion, after another Carol, they went into the house to the party

It was a lovely time everyone enjoyed themselves .They had a barn dance with recorded music after which Beth gave out the presents. They all had one. It was a moonlit night and as the folks walked the mile into the village along the river bank they could be heard at the house singing Carols as they went. Beth had been disappointed that Jeremy had not been there, he must have been out working. She knew he was on call for three villages this Christmas but he had been invited for dinner tomorrow. It was almost 12 midnight when she locked the quiet room up. Coming up the track was Jeremy full of apologies; "But I could not miss my kiss under the mistletoe," there in the moon light he certainly didn't. Christmas day was a delight. All the guests got on so well together. They enjoyed their dinner all home reared and cooked, after a walk by the river during the afternoon they came back to enjoy the meal at night which was a buffet that all the ladies had helped to prepare. Stories were told of other Christmases and Jeremy told what it was like in Africa last year and something of his work, which was rather sobering. However all went to bed early really happy. Mary Jane and her mother were very pleased that it had turned out so much better than they expected when in London.

Father Joseph came for several rest days after Christmas, for a time of peace and refreshment. Beth and he had times of prayer and reading the Bible together, prayed about the future of the Home how God wanted to use it. The visitors began to go home on various days after Christmas, or the first of January. Only the staff were in residence. No children were coming in January, this was to be a time of spring-cleaning, stocking the pantry with new stores more importantly – staff holidays, they were ready for a well-earned rest.

Beth had given Mary's mother, Grace, the housekeeping to do. At first she was so timid but well able to do it. Beth had given them quite a large room, en suite, with a small sink and cupboard, in which they could, if they wished, be private and have the odd meal by themselves.

During January the accountant came and the committee all sat round the table to see how they were doing. The guests had all contributed although they were not asked to do so. The sale of the eggs and autumn produce was more than satisfying. Peter said, "Next year we shall see better figures because we shall grow a lot more, I shall have to have more help, I think two more people if I am to be sharing the care of the youngsters as I have done up to now. I love having them and they have furthered my education as Cambridge never could even if I have gone there," everybody laughed heartily. "We are having plastic tunnels for growing early tomatoes and strawberries, would it be sensible this time to have youngsters a bit older who would like to work with me if I taught them?"

"It is worth a try, how about you and I going up to London to the crypt and seeing how the land lies? There may be someone looking for that kind of work but still we must carry on with holidays as well," Beth replied. The coffee and cakes came in then and stories were exchanged, the funny things the children had said were real entertainment.

Beth and Peter went to London and did what Beth had suggested. She saw some of the children who had already been, also some who were to come! After interviewing several, two sensible lads agreed to it a try on one month's trial. One was a country boy who thought the London streets were 'paved with gold', but could not get work or anywhere to live when his money had gone. Matthew and Paul joined the household.

One day on a walk with the children Beth found a man fishing in the river. This stretch was theirs to give permits to or hire them out, "Good morning I don't think we have met before do you have a permit to fish here?"

"I have been fishing here for years and do not need permission why do you ask?" he said.

"Because this is my land and you are trespassing and this mile long stretch of river goes with the house." Beth was not going to be put off by his next question

"Are these all your children, five of them?"

"Now stop changing the subject," she said. "I have children on holiday here and some of the boys would like to learn to fish and we have no fishermen in our household, so how about you coming to give them a lesson and let them sit beside you?"

"Oh yes I would like that, my grandchildren live miles away. I see very little of them, that would suit me a treat, when can I start? My name's Albert by the way."

"You can come up to the house tomorrow after we have had a talk you can do the fishing up by the house, the old Manor House now called Alpha Home." And with that she bade him Good day. She would have to ring the police officer and make sure he was a fit person to be with children, he seemed genuine enough and they would be outside the front door fishing!

Beth told the rest of the household before going to bed that night, at the usual chocolate time in the kitchen.

There had been some snow in January and very cold winds. February promised slightly better weather. There were only 20 sheep, and they were in the barn owing to the snow, but 18 of them would be producing lambs. Paul and Matthew settled in well although it was winter both appreciated a warm bed and regular food, in return they worked hard with Peter setting seeds in the 'tunnels' and preparing for the births in the barn.

Beth was seeing Jeremy occasionally. They were good friends by this time after a sticky start. Jeremy's time was now getting short he was due back in Africa at Easter time. Beth had mixed feelings about this, she knew in her heart she had met this person who Jake, her husband told her that one day she would meet and fall in love, with but how could anything become of this relationship when he was not of her faith. She did not want him to say he was a Christian because he wanted to marry her that would not do; well he had not asked her yet!!

There was a message from him on her return home that day. Would she spend the afternoon and evening with him on Saturday please? He had to go to the university in Cardiff and would like her go with him. Yes she would

Chapter 8

Beth spent the next two days wondering what to wear. She settled on dark jeans with a white polo sweater, boots fur lined and a red anorak. If they were going to the university she had better try and look like a student a thirty plus year old one.

It was a lovely spring day, as they drove over the hills the lambs were playing in the fields, the daffodils and bluebells were making their appearances in the woodlands, the bare branches of the trees were showing the slightest green sheen, soon the leaves would follow. Beth felt really happy and yet a tinge of sadness when she realised this was to be their last outing together before Jeremy went to Africa. Beth did some shopping in Cardiff whilst Jake went to the University to hand in his dissertation; the research was almost finished, only one more year. When he had begun this work he did not think he would be reluctant to leave England for the last year, he could not get to Africa fast enough four years ago.

They had a walk round the bay before finding a good hotel in which to have dinner. They settled themselves in a corner of the spacious lounge with a pot of coffee and began to talk. "Beth I really want to know what makes you 'tick'. Why did you give your inheritance to start the Alpha Home, when you could have lived in luxury for the rest of your life?"

"It is a long story but I will tell you if you want to know," she replied. "When I was eighteen I left the farm to go to London to be a nurse. Being in a big teaching hospital was a very lonely place. However I eventually made friends although it was not easy, the girl's name was Rachel and every Sunday she went to church when she was off duty. She was a kind loving girl and invited me to go with her; eventually I went having run out of excuses not to go! They had a course called the Alpha course running every Wednesday for ten weeks with a meal beforehand a video talk and discussion group afterwards. I thought this was not my scene really but every Wednesday I seemed to be off duty in the evening, in spite of myself I found myself ready to go. It was there I heard that Jesus died on the cross for the forgiveness of my sin, and by faith which was given to me by the Holy Spirit I became a Christian. Alpha means first, first means a new life, that's why I called the home Alpha because I want it to be the beginning of a new life for many people who live and work there. Being a Christian makes me want to help others into the Kingdom of God to enjoy the peace which He gives."

"Beth I only wish I could share your faith. After what I have dealt with in Africa, and having seen the suffering of children, I can't believe God is a loving God."

"I do understand you Jeremy, but God has given every one a free will to live as they please. If people choose to sleep around, become promiscuous when God gave us the Ten Commandments to live by, we can hardly blame Him when they take no notice of them and become infected. Sin can be forgiven but we often have to deal with the consequences. Which might be ill health, in some cases prison, or in a thousand ways, but God is there to help us, as when my parents died, I hope He has brought good out of that. Anyway you know now what makes me tick! I am going to miss you have you got another doctor for us?"

"Yes and you will be surprised who it is, your old friend, Dr Jenkins. I know you will be pleased. He is coming out of retirement for one year and then I am coming back to work here. Possibly to start a development programme in the village, building a health centre. And developing community care, of which you will be delighted to hear," he proudly told her.

"Oh, Jeremy, how wonderful, I shall eagerly look forward to that and you coming back to the village!" This was great news to Beth. It took a bit of the sting away from him going

"This brings me to my next question. I hardly dare ask you because I do not want to mess up our friendship. But, Beth, I do love you and hate leaving you, while I don't ask you to do so before I leave, but at least give me hope that one day you will marry me?" he said hopefully holding her hand.

"Jeremy, you do me the highest honour and I love you so much, but I can't marry you because we are not one in our faith. I know you think it will not matter but to me it will. I would not want you to become a Christian just to marry me, but if ever you do then the answer will be yes. In spite of myself I love you dearly and pray that one day we will be married."

"Come, Beth, our table is ready, this is nearly an engagement. The other thing I had to ask you have you got a room I could have at Easter weekend I am leaving on Easter Sunday evening, two weeks away now, but have to vacate the house before then.

"Jeremy, you know you can, do you want to come earlier? You are most welcome."

It was a very happy meal. Two happy people drove home. This was their last outing before Jeremy left, He had lots to do and pack for a year during the next two weeks.

The next week Beth had been giving the little girls a cookery lesson in the kitchen. They loved making fairy cakes for tea and got a lot of praise from the workers who enjoyed them. Paul came into the kitchen to say there was a man looking for Beth. He had been sent down from the farm. "Take him into the conservatory Paul and I will be there soon." She left the girls with Kate, washed her hands and went into the conservatory, to her amazement came face to face with Jake.

"Where on earth have you come from Jake? This is a surprise I have never heard from you for three years at least."

"I thought it was time that I paid you a visit, lady bountiful, is this all yours? I saw you had sold the farm, not delivering sheep anymore but organising other people to do the dirty work now, but who are all these people around the place?" enquired Jake.

"We are not always as throng as this but we have a small conference here for Easter Weekend. Normally we have children for holidays every fortnight from London. Remember Father Joseph? He sends me children who need a break and I love having them," she replied.

"Does the invitation extend to ex-husbands? Or nearly husbands? I am not staying long around here just a few nights if you will have me."

"Jake, you left me, remember? I have written two letters and you have not replied, you made it clear our relationship was over. However if you will have the room over the stables, I keep that free in case of someone needing it; you are welcome to it otherwise the house is full. Come to the kitchen, Paul will show you to the room and the evening meal is at 6.30p.m. We will talk after supper; I am busy now." Visibly shocked she went up to her sitting room followed by Julie who had heard the whole conversation.

"Beth, I heard all that, I am sorry, I always wondered about your husband but no one liked to ask you."

"I am so glad you came up, Julie, I feel quite shaken," she then told Julie the whole story; she was pleased to be able to talk to someone near to her. Julie was like a daughter to her and one who understood.

Dinner time was the usual merry time, lots of jokes, although the girls were much quieter than the boys. Paul and Matthew ate with them as did Kate and Bill who were both astonished to see Jake.

After dinner, Beth took Jake to the office where there were two easy chairs, but Beth sat at the desk. There was a knock at the door and Jeremy put his head round.

"I have brought my bag in Beth," said Jeremy, coming in through the door. "I am going to Sheila Jones, who is in labour. Are you going to introduce me to your visitor?"

"Jeremy, this is my ex-husband. Jake, this is our local doctor who is leaving us this weekend to go back to Africa," Beth introduced them.

"Hi Jake, enjoy your stay. I hope to be back before the night time but you never know how long these babies are going to take to make their way into the world. I will take a key in case it is during the night when I come back. When my year in Africa is over I am coming back to work in these villages as their GP and see how many other lame ducks Beth has collected, not the river variety!" He then rushed out of the house.

"He is staying here until he goes, has had to give his house up to the doctor who is taking over whilst he is away."

"So why have you come, Jake, and where have you been all this time? Did it work out in Canada? Did you go to South Africa to see your mum?"

"It is a long story, Beth. When I left you I went to Canada where I worked on my cousin's ranch, I then went to America to do the same, but it was too much like hard work. I then crewed on a ship going to South Africa. I did see my parents and told them I was married but they still did not want to know me. I then worked on an uncle's farm in Uganda. It was all hard work and little pay at the end of it. Eventually I found myself in the Mediterranean and wandered round Spain. I met a really good fellow who worked in a vineyard, had been there for 10 years and really enjoyed it. The owner was due to retire and putting the vineyard up for sale. I went along to meet him and stayed there for several weeks working amongst the vines. I might as well come to the reason I am here and that is to ask if you would like to invest in the vineyard, or make me a loan which would be repayable when we got on our feet so to speak. He is a similar type to me and we get along so well together, good companions. You never have signed the divorce papers of our marriage of convenience. With all this I should think that I am entitled to half of your money?"

"You cannot be serious, Jake, you leave me for years without a word and then come back expecting money from me? You should have told me what you were like before we were married. I must see my solicitor before I do anything. I have very little money in my account, this is all tied up in a charity and we are hoping this year to be self-sufficient. It is getting late now so go to bed. I will pray about this and hope to get an answer."

Beth felt very shaken and decided to wait up for Jeremy, to discuss it with him. She did not have long to wait, together they made hot chocolate in the kitchen before going to Beth's sitting room to try and sort this new problem out.

"You must not give him anything, Beth, I have not asked anything about him before but now I have seen him I don't need to. Men like him do not need their lifestyle funding. See your solicitor, you don't owe him anything. Go to bed now, I wish I could say come to bed but I can't. Good night, my darling," and with that he walked quickly down the corridor.

Easter Saturday was a lovely day. The weather was perfect, the river flowing rapidly, the woodland trees were just bursting into bud, the Flowering Cherry trees were in full bloom as were the spring flowers and bluebells. Some guests took sandwiches and walked round the hills, others went to Swansea to the sea side. Julie's parents took her, Jamie and Peter out for the day, whilst Beth, Mary and her Mother did the cooking and fed the chickens, helped by the children.

It was a merry meal that night all seated round the table. Beth had cooked a turkey with lots of Vegetables followed by the favourite apple pie and cream. Jeremy said goodbye to everyone after supper in case he did not see them in the morning. He was leaving his car there in case it was needed. He and Beth spent the last evening together. Her heart was nearly breaking when at last they said good night.

She showered and got into bed when the door gently opened and Jeremy came and slid into bed beside her. She quickly slid into his arms saying, "We should not be doing this." Their love making was gentle and so satisfying. He could not believe this was her first time, but having seen her husband he was not surprised. Sleep was forgotten they loved and talked most of the night until the dawn broke; one night of love was worth all the years of frustration she had previously endured.

Jeremy quickly showered and dressed and they went to the kitchen to make breakfast. Beth was taking him to the station for the early train to London for the evening flight to Kenya. The rest of the day passed in a dream. They went to church for the Easter morning service, made Easter bonnets in the afternoon, and in the evening went into the quiet place and sang Easter hymns: A wonderful day. On Monday the guests started to return home and the next lot of boys arrived for their holiday.

Chapter 9

The following week two significant things happened.

Jake was wanting to be off but he would not go until he had some money. They went to the solicitor who made some enquiries by telephone, actually speaking to the Vineyard owner and finding it was true what Jake had said. They then agreed to let him have £10,000 as an investment and down payment on the property. The solicitor wrapped it all up very well leaving no loopholes where Beth could be swindled. Jake was then on the next train to town!

"Are you glad I went away now? You can have a taste of what real love is like; that doctor looked as if he could eat you for dinner last night, are you going to marry him?" he asked her.

"Not unless he becomes a Christian, and just because he wants me to marry him, but yes I am very fond of him. He has gone away for a year now anyway. Goodbye, Jake, I might just come over and see our little bit of the vineyard one day. We will see how it goes." She was glad to see him go but also pleased that they had not fallen out and he had got what he wanted; or at least some of it!!"

The second was a letter from Jeremy again, unexpected. It was a long letter so she went into the summer house to read its very surprising contents.

My darling, Beth. All the way to London I felt guilty that I had never told you about my past marriage just as you had not told me about Jake. That was however rectified so that now I am telling you about my 'mistake'. There was a society woman patient who I fell in love with. She was beautiful, we had dinner together on several occasions, and although she was engaged she said she loved me, too. The wedding was arranged; a marquee on the lawn and all the trimmings. A month before the wedding she met me without the ring on. 'I have been jilted, Jeremy, will you marry me?' I was so taken aback, she did not want to lose face at the wedding and thought what we had for each other would be enough. Looking back I was more than a fool. We had the big wedding; her parents thought little of a humble doctor for a son-in-law but she was a determined woman. I will not bore you with the details but after two years of more or less going our own way I opened a letter one day by mistake, it was a letter from a Harley Street Specialist who had performed an abortion on her and sent a hefty bill. I packed my bags and was just leaving when she came in; she said she did not want to look pregnant and lose her figure, apparently it was a boy. I was completely devastated that she would do that without telling me. That was the end for me. After the divorce she married the consultant who had aborted her; he was an old friend of mine. I became a very bitter man that is why I eventually took on this AIDS programme. You said when I went to the Alpha Home you were going to chisel the chip off my shoulder and, my dearest Beth, you have certainly done that. I feel free of bitterness now although I cannot accept your faith. Please pray that one day I might 'see the light,' I would like to. Your loving Jeremy.

Beth sat on in the summer house feeling surprised at the letter. She was pleased that he had the courage to send it; at least she now understood how he had been when he first spoke to her on the telephone at Julie's confinement. She imagined how he must have felt holding little Jamie in his arms and examining him. 'Lord please forgive us for our night of love, I know it is wrong outside marriage, but it was so lovely.' The thought came to Beth. God forgives sin but the consequences have to be dealt with sometimes. Little did she know what these were going to be. Back in the office with Rebecca life went on as normal.

The next milestone was Jamie's birthday. He was such a happy little boy, always smiling and loving all the animals when Peter took him round the field. Beth enjoyed looking after him but Peter idolised him. One day he was trying to say Mum, Mum, Peter said; "say Dad, Dad."

"Peter, what are you doing? When Julie marries he will have to get used to another Dad, Dad."

"He won't you know because I am going to marry Julie," he sounded so confident.

"Does she know yet?" Beth was quite amused at this turn of events. She could tell they were very fond of each other and would make a lovely couple.

"Don't you tell her before I do," he warned her, "after all I was holding her hand when he was born. So I should have the first refusal!!"

"We will have a first birthday party for him on second of June, if you are quick about it you can get engaged at the same time, maybe a double celebration."

"Now you are putting thoughts into my head, do you think she will say yes?"

The committee came together for the end of first year meeting. As usual the coffee and biscuits were on the table as well as a lot of good humour. After prayer to open the proceedings Beth gave her report. She was complimented on the running of the home and the Christmas party as well as the Easter weekend which was enjoyed by all. Would she give a special thanks to the staff? The fact that the guests had largely paid for their stay made the accountant happy. Now Beth what are your plans for the coming year?"

"We hope to continue giving holidays to the youngsters in London, also anyone else who would like to come. Father Joseph has been asking if we could take a couple of drug addicts and treat them. They are a young man and his girlfriend who go to his crypt and are longing to get off drugs. I have no real knowledge of this kind of treatment so it would be up to you doctor to say if you think this would be appropriate for us to do. The boy has been to drama school and unfortunately been with friends of the wrong kind where he has met the girlfriend. He wants to get back into acting again. I will depend on your judgement on this one," said Beth.

"Let me think about this, Beth, the only danger of helping drug addicts in the long term is the 'pushers', they might find out where they are and try to get them back onto taking drugs, however we are remote enough here for that not to happen, I think."

Several days after the meeting he rang to say let's give it a try; we will work on them together. The next week, May and Gerald arrived looking pale and lifeless but determined to kick the habit.

August 1st saw the first year over. Again they had a party and thanksgiving service. The buffet was served outside the conservatory by the river which sparkled in the sunshine; Jamie now was walking around being admired by all the guests.

Beth had been feeling "fragile" in the mornings, not being able to eat certain foods because of indigestion. She went to the village to see the doctor who was a good friend, "It would seem you are pregnant, Beth." She almost fainted with shock. "Just think back to Easter your husband turned up for almost a week could it have happened then? I would be surprised if it did but stranger things have happened," he said, knowing Jake.

Beth's face flamed and tears ran down her face. He took her into his lounge for coffee and said if she wanted to confide in him she could depend on him keeping to himself any confidences. An hour later she felt so much better, having shared with him who the father really was. She did not want Jeremy to know of the pregnancy until after the birth considering his earlier disappointment in his marriage.

. The summer progressed happily. Outside activities flourished. May and Gerald, determined to come clean, spent a lot of time outside and began to look much better, and help around the house. Beth's bump was beginning to show, although she had shared with Kate and Julie they were the only ones who knew the whole truth. When she went to the post office the next week taking Jamie for a walk she stood outside the open door and heard Nellie saying to a customer, "Well what do you know, that Jake turns up for one week and clears off again and leaves Beth in that condition."

"Well," said Ada, "I never did trust him, a nice enough chap but there was sommat a bit shifty about him. She has mothered all those kids from London now she will know what it's like to be a real mother. She is a lovely girl."

Beth walked away she could not go into the shop right then!! Let them think it was Jake's child, when it was born they would know to whom it belonged.

Chapter 10

In Africa Jeremy's thoughts were often in Wales. His research team were working in a small village in quite primitive accommodation. The office was a concrete building, fortunately with air conditioning. Their bedrooms were in a similar building with little by the way of air conditioning. A lounge and dining room where the six of them lived and worked when not out in the field collecting samples and giving out medicines. Three women and three men. The older woman was a real research boffin who was bossy efficient and determined that everyone should know it! The other two were gentler types with several failed relationships and both were very fond of Jeremy. They were not best pleased when he came back from England with a gold-framed photograph of a lovely blond girl laughing up at him as if sharing a joke.

"It looks as though we are too late," Nichola said. She looks a nice person, I think she was good for him, he has been much better tempered since he came back, even smiles more, not that there is a lot to smile about in this job."

They did research in pairs around far flung villages giving out medicines and examining babies and adults. To see if the medicines had taken effect over the years. It could be lonely work so that when they were near to towns they tried to see a film or some entertainment. Outside a church on their way home one day they saw advertised an Alpha Course due to start the next night. This was only two miles from their living accommodation, Jeremy stopped and took the telephone number down. The name was so familiar so for that alone he thought it would be something to do.

The next night found him sitting with about twelve people round a table eating rice and chicken before seeing the video explaining who God was, then having a discussion group afterwards. He quite enjoyed arguing with the minister in a friendly way and as the weeks progressed he was becoming more warm hearted to the Lord, although being of a stubborn nature he would not accept totally what was being said, until the 'Holy Spirit night' when it was explained that after Jesus rose from the dead. He sent the Holy Spirit to be in the disciples, not with them as He had been in person, but to be a force in their lives to empower them to become the leaders of Christianity as we know it today. He was like a can of petrol standing beside a car that had run out of fuel, it would not go whilst it was in the can but once the petrol was in the car it could be driven at any speed. That is like some Christians, they do not know the power of the Holy Spirit because they will not believe what He can do for a person. We only have to ask Him sincerely and He will do for us what we ask Him and what we need.

Jeremy was strangely moved. As he drove home along unmade roads he stopped and prayed, 'Lord please make your Spirit help me to believe.' Immediately a warm glow suffused his body, and he found he was saying words which he did not understand, and a longing to know more. The old bitterness drained out of him and he was filled with joy and peace that he had never before experienced. There close on midnight he sang the only song he knew; 'Praise my soul the king of heaven'! How he wished Beth could be here with him now to share in his joy.

When he got in the accommodation the others were still up. He came in smiling and they asked if he had been drinking. "No not that kind of spirit." He was longing to tell Beth but he did not want her to think it was just to marry her; this was for real.

Back home in Wales Beth was struggling a bit. It was the end of October now the nights were darker and the weather cooler. She could not move about as quickly feeling increasing discomfort. The boys who were there this fortnight were a law unto themselves. Occasionally the children were so used to doing what they liked on the streets they did not take happily to having boundaries. One big problem was the river, fast flowing although not too deep; the small current could sweep them downstream easily. Some well-meaning soul bought a dinghy which was hidden round the cow shed. One afternoon, two boys, unknown to anyone else, took the dinghy out on the river and were washed down stream. One of the fishermen saw them and raised the alarm. The boys were thrown out when it capsized and Peter and Gerald were working in a field near the river and fortunately rescued them. They had swallowed a lot of water, the doctor was called and the ambulance, which resulted in a trip to the hospital in Swansea. They were kept in overnight; seeing as though there was no real damage they were discharged the next day. It had nevertheless shaken Beth; such a thing had, surprisingly, never happened before."

The Harvest thanksgiving went very well. The villagers came for the Harvest supper followed by a Barn Dance enjoyed by all. May and Gerald were not dependent on drugs anymore and were looking better.

Father Joseph came down for a week's break. Walking in the woods and meditating in the quiet room. Beth confided in him the parentage of the expected baby. Although he does not know about the baby he asked me to marry him, I said I love him dearly but cannot be married if we were not one in the faith, I would rather be a single parent." said Beth.

"God will answer your prayers, Beth, have a little more faith, He will work it out."

The preparations for Christmas were going ahead although Beth was very tired buying all the presents wrapping them and buying in extra stores for the meals.

It was the morning of Christmas Eve. Beth did not feel right, there were little 'feelings' rippling around her stomach, which by dinner time became stronger. She went in search of Peter. "Could you drive me to Swansea, please, I think the baby has started."

"I had better call someone else; I don't want to deliver you by the roadside on my own! Are we making a habit of meeting at deliveries? Shall I hold your hand as well?" they were both laughing when they asked Kate if she could come, the others could get on with the food. Mary's mother was a good cook so they were well served.

Peter was shouting, "Come on, Beth, you need to get there quickly and it is a bumpy road which might hurry you on," holding the door open for them to get in. "Have you got all that you need"?

By the time they arrived at the hospital Beth was well on in labour, she went straight into the delivery suite and one hour later she was delivered of a sweet little baby girl. Peter was holding her hand! And Jane was at the other side in her mother's place. Seeing that it was a straightforward birth, several hours later, on Christmas morning, she was sent home by ambulance to the local midwife.'

There was a reception committee on the front doorstep, "Beth you do everything for us even provide a baby on Christmas morning!"

There were hugs and kisses all round in thanksgiving for the new life. "I have been the stand-in father at two baby's births and neither have been mine," Pete told them all. Julie ran up to him, "Well the next one will be I am sure because we are getting engaged today." There were cheers all round and even champagne in the lounge, what a happy day.

Beth said, "Please let us think of Jeremy in Africa, this darling child is his, and he has no idea she was coming. I just wish he was here to see her." She then went in to put through a call to Africa to tell him the good news, but he was not there.

Meanwhile in Africa Jeremy was languishing on a sick bed in the hospital. He had been in a village for several days and forced to eat the native food. Although he did not like it he was hungry and forced to eat it. Fortunately his partner did not eat it and so drove him to hospital curled up in the foetal position in the back of the Land Rover. "If having a baby is half as bad as this I am glad that I am a man." Little did he know that Beth was going through the same thing in England.

Jeremy was admitted to hospital. He was given a saline drip and sedated for several days, he was extremely ill. He knew how ill he was. He asked for the pastor of the Alpha church to come and pray for him. God heard his prayer and began the healing process. His life was saved, this was Christmas Eve, the night his daughter was born. Two weeks later he was out of hospital convalescing, not strong enough to fly home.

During this time Beth was frantic with worry. Her phone calls were answered by a female voice saying he had a stomach bug, was in hospital and would contact her on his return. Eventually he was able to speak to Beth and suggested she could fly out to the Maldives for a week's holiday and he would meet her there. He did not want to go to England in February, after the Maldives he only had to go back for two months to finish the research project he had been working on He made all the arrangements for Beth, she only had to get on the aircraft and go!

The baby who she had called Elizabeth was going to stay with Kate and Bill whilst she was away. The Island they were going to was Villamendoo an idyllic island reached only by sea plane. One hotel on the island but all around the perimeter were brick bungalows with their own little beach, fringed with trees for shade. This indeed was paradise.

Before he went he bought two rings hoping they would be married on this Island. They had a lot to share, Beth hoped that it would all work out right. They both had secrets to tell the other.

Beth was happy that she was leaving the Home in good safe hands. Bill in charge of the animals, Peter the market garden, Kate in charge of the home, Marys Mother the cooking and Jason – the curate from London – coming to care for the children he was bringing with him. So it was a light-hearted Beth that boarded the aircraft to take her to Mahle and by sea plane to the Paradise Island.

Jeremy was waiting for her on the landing stage in Mahle; they flew into each other's arms and were so pleased to be together again. They were given a bungalow with twin beds. The first night after dinner they told their stories. Jeremy could not believe he was a father at last, she showed him her photograph and his tears dropped on it! Then he told of his conversion and the Alpha course he had attended and how excited he had become on the way home after receiving the gift of the Holy Spirit. There was such rejoicing on that island and praise to God, it was wonderful.

The Islands were like lily pads resting on the ocean. For about 100 metres from the beach the water was shallow and as they waded into the water the thousands of tiny brilliantly coloured fishes swam round their legs, not a bit afraid of them. Further out a deep drop into the ocean revealed the coral reef, it had to be seen to be believed.

The wedding was to be on the Thursday. Other holiday makers were to be witnesses and although it was not a particularly religious affair they would have their proper wedding back home. Beth wore a swim suit covered by a sarong and they stood on the beach in brilliant sun shine along with so many guests who had come to wish them well. The chaplain of the islands came to bless them and their joy was complete.

Their week of paradise was over all too soon. With an early call on the morning of departure they walked onto .the Jetty to board the boat which took them to the pontoon where the little sea plane had been secured all night. The sea all around them was turquoise blue, calm and serene in the early morning light. The two other passengers in the boat were the pilots to fly them to Mahle. It was interesting to see the pilots checking the plane and putting petrol in it from a can! Beth's plane took off first to fly to London via Dubai Jeremy could hardly let her go, he longed to be going to see his daughter. Beth waved out of the window then suddenly she was alone and on her way. Jeremy had several hours to wait before he was airborne.

What a welcome she received at The Alpha House, she did not realise how much she was loved; she just held up her left hand and let her third finger give the message!

'All things work together for good to those who love God, those who are called according to His purpose,' this was a text which came into her mind as she flew home. This time she had proved it to be true again.

She invited them all to come into the quiet room to hear what she had to say. "You will be pleased to hear I am now Mrs Beth Johnson." Holding up her left hand she then proceeded to tell them of Jeremy's illness and how much weight he had lost, but more so about his conversion at the Alpha Course in the African village church. How they had enjoyed times of fellowship on the island and here are the photographs to prove it. Her shining face was enough to give them all the proof they needed. Our wedding blessing will be at Easter time in the village Church. Jeremy will be coming back as our doctor and developing patient care in the community." She was so pleased to tell them.

The next morning Beth made her way to the office where there was a phone call for her. A person calling from Cardiff saying he had met Jeremy at the university, he had told him there were a bunch of weirdoes who accepted anyone who wanted peace and quiet to stay for a while.

"I think you had better come and see these weirdoes Mr."

"Call me Old Nick, I am a doctor, actually, and needing to write a thesis. Nick told me about the valiant work you are doing there amongst needy people and I thought you might take pity on me."

"When do you want to come?"

"At the weekend for about six weeks. I can well afford to pay for my stay, in my spare time perhaps help in some way, either in the market garden or the farm. By the way have you heard from Jeremy lately?" he asked.

"I have just got back from the Maldives where we have been to get married. He has been desperately ill in Africa over Christmas, but I can tell you about it when we meet. Until the weekend then, Nick, good bye."

"He sounds as if he will be an asset to the Home she said to Rebecca."

Old Nick arrived. He looked the most disreputable character she had ever met. His clothes were torn and not very clean, he had walked a long way; not much luggage just a back pack. Beth was so surprised but tried not to show it. His hands however were beautiful, long fingers and well-manicured nails, quite out of keeping to the rest of him. He seemed to have a good sense of humour, crinkly eyes when he smiled.

"My name is Nicholas Poynton, but they call me Old Nick. I take after the devil," he tried to shock her.

"We welcome you, Nick, but we don't have devils here if we can help it," she laughingly told him. "So perhaps you can work on it! Come and have some coffee and I will show you round."

When they got to the quiet room he wanted to know why they needed a chapel. Beth told him about her parents and that this was not basically a church but a quiet place where he could do his work and also it was a library.

Gerald showed Nick to his room after which they both came down to good old stew and dumplings followed by sponge cake and custard. Which was enjoyed by all. Beth went up for the story, they had had four new boys in that day and she needed to supervise their hair washing, etc. When they were in bed she told them the rules of the Home and how those disobedient boys nearly got drowned in the river." I am sure if you do what we say you are going to have a lovely time. You can help on the farm, or the market garden, collect the eggs and wash them, feed the hens. So many things to do.

"Please, Miss, I fort we had come for a holiday not to work," concern showing in his young face.

These things are not work, Rick, it's seeing things you don't have in London. It is time for lambs to be born and when a birth is about to take place Bill will ring a bell and those who want to can go to see it. We have to be quiet so as not to upset the mother sheep. Then Peter will milk the cow who gives us milk to drink. You are going to have a lovely time, boys. Off to sleep now who would like a kiss?"

"Kissing is for lasses, Miss. Nobody kisses me."

"Good night then," said Beth. "Sleep well"

Easter was looming ahead, Beth went to see her friend the vicar.

"About the blessing, shall we have it in the village Church or down at the House?"

"The village people would like it here I am sure, Beth. They have known you all their lives, and your parents, it would be nice to include them all in the celebrations. You could have the reception at the house, they would all go down for that, but the quiet place is not big enough to get everyone in," he said. The date was fixed for Easter Sunday after the morning service.

Beth took Kate and Julie shopping into Swansea to buy wedding clothes; once again they laughed about it and loved every minute of it.

"This is getting to be a habit Beth! I hope this is the last time you are going to be married," said Kate.

Julie was to be bridesmaid, Kate the bride's Mother. Bill would 'give her away'. She bought invitations to send out to relatives, she had already told Uncle John and Kenneth, she reminded herself to ask Jeremy for his parents address. He did not mention them at all, but they must be invited even if she did not meet them beforehand.

Nick settled in very well. They did not see much of him when he was not in the quiet room he was in the woods, which were looking particularly good with spring flowers and bluebells in bud, the birds nesting and some water hens building nests by the river bank. Beth also walked in the woods whenever she could spare the time to take the children there. Some took to the farm and country life very well, others were afraid of the animals, even the hens.

In March, Beth had three girls and three boys down at the same time. They obviously had different dormitories, but each knew where the others were sleeping.

The same rules applied to both sexes although the girls were a bit younger than the boys. Tom was one of the boys, he was very naughty and disobedient at times .He had been told about the river event when the boys had taken the boat out and the consequences. He loved showing off in front of the girls, frightened them with ghost stories, but the final straw came when he put frogs in two of their beds.

Peter and Beth had him in the office "Why are you behaving like this, Tom, you are causing so much unhappiness to these girls they want to go home."

"It is only a bit of fun hearing them squeal is a laugh."

"Well look out because if you think that this is fun you are in for a shock .You are not only older than them but bigger as well, so you should know better. If your behaviour does not improve you will have to go home on the train alone and see how brave you are then, Beth tried not to get angry.

Tom looked quite shocked, "You can't make me do that, Miss, I would not know where to go."

"Well you know you have to behave properly and say sorry to the girls, little Sally gets a lot of bullying from her big brother, she was looking forward to being here without him and now you have taken his place! If you say sorry she might just forgive you. We all do wrong things, Tom, and have to ask God to forgive us as well as the ones we hurt, we will have a story about that tonight."

He went off still not saying sorry; he thought he had been 'got at', how did his mother cope with a family like that? Fortunately they were not used to having to chastise the children they were normally well behaved. Odd ones had done some things, like letting the cows out into the lane with manure all in the wrong places. Bill gave them a shovel and made them take it to the garden to Peter after collection. All kinds of practical jokes on the staff were tolerated. Nick said he was surprised the staff put up with so much hassle so good humouredly. When some of them became swearing and rude Beth just said, "We do not swear here and we respect other people. If you continue to swear we shall get the washing up liquid out and wash out your Mouth." That had a dramatic effect on them usually, they had not carried out the threat do date. The difference in two weeks was amazing, good food and fresh air, someone to take an interest in them and a good night kiss worked wonders.

The second week in April Jeremy came home, what a welcome he got. Balloons out, welcome home posters, and a big party. The preparations for the wedding went ahead and Jeremy felt he had to go and see his parents in London before the big day. He was surprised to see Old Nick there still, his thesis was finished, but he could not tear himself away! He, too, had changed; instead of sneering at the work going on there he actually felt the peace of the place and spent most of his time when not with the children in the quiet room.

Chapter 11

The day of the wedding dawned fine and sunny. Beth fed Elizabeth and Jamie in the kitchen after breakfast. Outside caterers were doing the reception which took the pressure off the staff. Jeremy's parents were coming to meet Beth at 11.0a.m., the day before the wedding. Jeremy was besotted with his daughter, nursing her whenever she was awake. Jamie was always around Beth because she had cared for him so much. She was almost like his mother.

The Church was decorated with flowers on every ledge and the end of every pew. Wall flowers, freesias. Heavily scented lilies perfumed the whole Church. Beth wore an ankle-length lace dress of the palest lavender with a white slip underneath and white accessories. Julie was in palest pink and white whilst Kate was in a grey silk dress and jacket, so suitable for the bride's mother, just what her mum would have chosen. Bill was the proudest man in Wales that day, walking down the aisle with the prettiest lady on his arm, certainly not looking her 35 years.

Their vows were spoken with such sincerity, the hymns resounded around the walls and steeple and everyone was happy and rejoicing. Kenneth could not get away from his practice that weekend to give her away. They were coming down for a holiday later in the summer.

The reception went really well, there was a happy atmosphere; around 80 guests wished them well and thanked them both for their work in the area. Jeremy had three weeks to settle in before he became their doctor again. Beth then went up to her sitting room to spend some time with her husband's parents. Jeremy brought in Elizabeth and presented her to his father, their first grandchild.

Looking back the next day on the time spent with Jeremy's parents she understood why he had not talked about them. The first thing the mother said was, "Is this a shot gun wedding or do you love each other? The baby usually comes after the wedding not before."

"Mother you would not understand if we went into all the details. We have known each other since Beth set up this home and sold her farm. I was only here for one year before going back to Africa, but we fell in love and on the last night that I was here we yielded to temptation and our darling Elizabeth is the result. Beth did not tell me until well after she was born, so I would feel under no obligation to marry her."

"Are you sure she is your child?" she was determined to have the last word.

"How can you say such things; she even looks like me and if she was not mine I would still love her. I love Beth far more than ever words can say, after my last encounter with marriage I consider myself extremely fortunate in meeting Beth and I intend helping her in this work of bringing happiness to many lives and showing them there is a better way of life following our Lord Jesus."

She then looked round the room at the lovely furniture, ornaments and things from Beth's mother's home and asked her where she got them from.

"They were my mother's things we had in the farm I sold when they were killed in a coach crash in Spain. My mother's family owned a castle in Scotland before they died, but neither of their two sons wanted the estate and so it was sold and I expect this was some of the furniture they had."

"Why did you set this place up for down and outs when you could live in luxury for the rest of your lives?"

"Because I am a Christian, I worked in the Crypt in London giving out soup and a listening ear, and finding that one half does not know how the other half lives, and it is not always their fault they have no home. Jesus went around doing good for people and making a difference to their lives. He can change hardened hearts and bring forgiveness and restitution in families, I have seen wonderful reunions with some down and outs. I might say I have found some up and outs as well." Beth found it easy to talk to this embittered woman, strangely enough.

"I think you have brainwashed my son into your way of thinking, he used to be very different to what I find he is now."

Jeremy's father was a gentle man; whilst his wife was talking he was standing by the window looking at the river, cuddling Elizabeth in his arms. He was a consultant cardiologist in a London hospital. A very gentle man.

Beth was so pleased when they went home. It had been a long day. Before Jeremy's father left he told Beth if there was anything she needed just to let him know. He admired her and what she was doing, giving her a hug and kiss; she felt she had made a friend

The next week Jeremy was in London for several days winding up the research project. The new set of boys were outside types and had made a den in the woods by the river bank. Gerald, one of the boys, came running back on the Friday morning calling her name.

"Miss Beth, I have found a tramp lying in our den on some bracken and I thought I heard him moaning. The other lads are with him now."

She went into the kitchen, made sandwiches and a flask of Horlicks, and quickly followed Gerald back to the den. Sure enough the man looked like a tramp! A long beard, very matted hair, but clear blue eyes.

"Go and find Nick, Gerald, he is a doctor and will know what to do." As she was talking the man looked at her and asked who she was. "I am the owner of this land and have a house down the path. I would like you to come down and sleep in a better place, you are more than welcome to stay until you feel better."

I don't want to move, it is so peaceful here. I am warm with my blanket and just want to be left in peace please." He was well spoken and Beth felt there was a story behind this gentle man. Shortly Nick arrived with a medical bag and started asking questions.

"I am not here for long, young man. I have a cancer and don't want to be a burden to anyone with my problems." He did, however, enjoy the Horlicks and sandwiches. They introduced themselves and said they would come later if he changed his mind about coming to the house. He closed his eyes and they left him to sleep."

"We do have to accept people's feelings and independence," Beth said sadly to the boys. "We will keep an eye on him and speak to him later. Nick took his books into the wood and stayed away from him, out of his sight. Towards evening Beth brought more Horlicks and rice pudding. She brought a sleeping bag for Nick because he was going to spend the night with him. His name was Roger he said but would offer no more information about himself. During the night, however, he started to talk about himself to Nick who lay by his side. He had wife with a very extravagant lifestyle and two children who did not take any notice of anything he said. He was a teacher and could not control a class of hooligans who did not want to learn, and so felt a thorough failure." He got very emotional after this and Nick did not know how to handle it.

"If Beth were here she would say let us pray about it. I cannot do that but I do know the Lord 's Prayer, let us say that together." They held hands and together recited "forgive us our debts as we forgive those who have wronged us," Roger meant that and felt a peace as if he had been forgiven as he forgave those who had brought him to the state he was in. Nick left him early in the morning to go and get some breakfast for them. Roger thanked him for the night and told him he was at peace with himself and the family.

After Nick had gone Roger left his jacket and belongings in the den and walked into the cold sparkling waters of the river and let them flow over him, he was at peace as he had never known it for a long time.

Nick raised the alarm when he found Roger was missing, he had floated downstream and was by the house when they took him out, and called the police. Nick and Beth were devastated. Beth took the boys to Swansea that day to get them out of the way of the police activity.

The details were in his jacket and his wife and two sons came to identify the body. He was not an old man at all, but the cancer had progressed without treatment and according to them it was the best way for him to go. Beth was not surprised that he had left home, they were down on him all right, they had not a good word to say about him, the poor chap.

Beth took the children down to the beach in Swansea to be away from the home when the Police came. The day at the seaside went down very well. It was warm enough to bathe. The sand castle competition was good Jamie enjoyed knocking them down after the judging. It was Elizabeth's first time to feel sand on her toes she kicked and laughed really entertaining the group; fish and chips out of paper culminated the day's pleasures and a very happy party became homeward bound. Beth had kept her eye on Gerald who had been subdued most of the day. When they got home Nick was waiting for them, they all three, Nick, Beth and Gerald, went into the quiet place, Nick brought them up to date and said the relatives were coming the next day.

"I found him, Miss, but it was not enough, could I have done more for him?" Gerald said with tears in his eyes. Beth then explained that he had cancer and did not want any treatment. Life had got him down.

"Do you know what one problem was, Gerald? He was a teacher and the kids in his class were hooligans and would not listen when he tried to teach them. He was a kind and gentle man so will you remember when you are playing up in class and giving the teacher a hard time you might be the cause of his break down? You are a born leader and can help your friends by telling them what happened to Roger." Nick replied.

He then went on to tell them what happened during the night and how in reciting the Lord's Prayer, forgiving and asking forgiveness Roger found peace in his heart and knew it was time to go. They all shed a few tears and Beth prayed that they would know the peace of the Lord that night. When she kissed Gerald good night he whispered "thank you, Miss, I wish you were my mum."

This incident had a big effect on Old Nick. He went to see Beth the next morning. "I do admire you so much, I wish I had your faith, I am quite envious of Jeremy coming back to a wife like you. This place has got hold of me, I do not want to leave but feel, after Roger, I should get away for a while to sort myself out."

"You old flatterer," she said. "He should be back in two days' time for good. Have you finished your work? You only came for four weeks originally."

"My work is finished. I love being here, should really get a job for the next six months or until I can make up my mind what I want to do. When I said the Lord's Prayer with Roger something seemed to happen inside me, I felt tremendous compassion for him, I am not used to these feelings and don't want to feel them. I am not into this Christian stuff. My parents were so strict with me as a boy, I have done my best to get rid of these feelings and I had until I came here. Yours is a different kind of Christianity it works for you." Nick was so sincere.

"But not for you?" asked Beth?

"No but we shall see, I have not seen my old folks for over a year up north so I think I shall visit them, you see you have had some good effect on me. I have loved this casual look but must get some decent clothes before I go there. I must confess I do not usually dress like this but Jeremy was telling me what you did here and I thought you would not welcome a tramp and did this to test you, sorry, Beth, you proved me wrong, that was the Old Nick in me coming out!

Nick left the next day. Beth took him to Swansea station and reluctantly said goodbye. She had come to depend on him quite a lot, but Jeremy would be home this week and she was greatly looking forward to that.

Chapter 12

The committee met together at their half yearly meeting. All was going well with the finances and Beth gave a report on the holidays. They were extremely sad about Roger committing suicide and Nick going away. Jeremy was back and at the meeting and due to start work in the village the next week. Once again it was time to say farewell to the old Doctor, although he was welcome to return any time he wanted. Beth reported that she was awaiting a large log cabin to make a proper tea room. The conservatory was very popular but not big enough. Kate was interviewing a couple to come and work at the home, after advertising, and sifting through the replies. Sally and John Rigley were coming to live in the village, Sally to take over the cafe and gift shop, John to be 'jack of all trades' to work wherever he was needed. The meeting closed with prayer and thanksgiving for the Lord's protection and blessing.

A week later the log cabin came trundling up the lane on the back of a lorry in two parts. It was so wide the trees were suffering! Branches being torn off. It was followed by a huge crane which lifted the cabin onto the prepared concrete footing. In no time at all it was bolted together, and we had a Cafe. Sally soon had it cleaned and carpeted, chintz curtains up with tables and chairs enough for about 40 people to dine in style. Peter brought plants and flowers from the greenhouses. The children were fascinated watching it all being built, arguing who would be the first to be served sandwiches and tea! The opening was to be on Sunday afternoon. The folks came from the village for the ceremony and free refreshments. Peter read from the Bible 'Except the

Lord build the house they labour in vain who made it.' Beth asked God to bless the shop and "all who eat and drink in it." By seven o'clock everyone had gone home or indoors.

A lovely June evening the birds were singing cows mooing, rabbits scurrying over the river bank and the little ducks quietly clucking, settling their little ones for the night. Beth and Jeremy went into the quiet place to give thanks to God for His goodness to them and all who worked at The Alpha Home.

During the night Jeremy became hot and restless, Beth had felt uneasy about his health since he had come home from Africa. He did not openly complain but was taking indigestion tablets by the box full! "Are you in pain Jeremy," she asked, getting out of bed.

"I am afraid so, darling it could be a bit like my old trouble in Africa when I was so ill, although I have not eaten anything to cause it this time, it could be a rouge infection that has lingered. The pain is getting worse, could you drive me to the hospital, Beth, or shall I get ask Peter?

Now Beth was really worried, Jeremy was pretty tough normally and did not realise how ill he had been in Africa. She got up and roused Julie to take care of the babies, Told Peter where she was going, asked that he take charge of the home in her absence, and as dawn was breaking they drove to the hospital in Swansea for advice. He was now sweating profusely and groaning with pain. He had felt twinges for several days but did not want to worry Beth.

He was admitted immediately and with his history put in an isolation room until they could identify the cause. He gave them his history of eating infected food, "But in the hovels where I had to work I could have caught anything, originally it was a chicken concoction which I had to eat because I was so hungry."

Beth reluctantly left him in hospital and went back home. She was very worried and called the old doctor who still was in the village to ask him to stay and cover for Jeremy. When you are nursing you are not so involved emotionally. "Now is the time to practice what you preach," she told herself, little did she know how much her faith was going to be tried.

The next morning a call from the hospital telling her to come at once was received. She made arrangements at the home to be away and took a night case with her not knowing what to expect. Jeremy was in the side ward with full isolation nursing procedures in practice. She gowned up, put on a mask, covered her head and went into the room. He was lying with his eyes closed semi-conscious. Beth sent a message to his parents putting them in the picture, although they were not allowed to visit at this stage. His only brother was in New Zealand and not likely to come.

Beth sat beside him praying for the Lord to heal him. He was getting weaker and until they had isolated the infection would not be able to treat him properly Beth stayed at the hospital mostly all through the next week. After two days they started some new drug which made some impression on his condition. His temperature came down slightly and by the end of the week he was sitting up in bed talking to Beth although still extremely weak.

Beth had been staying in hospital accommodation but was now able to go home in the evenings.

"I was just as ill as this in Africa, Beth. I remember saying if labour pains are as bad as this thank goodness I am a man, little did I know you were experiencing labour pains at the same time."

"Yes darling but look what my pains produced, our darling daughter, she was worth every pain. Peter rushed me to the hospital insisting Kate came as well in case he had to deliver me on the way! He was there holding Julie's hand when Jamie was born and likewise holding mine when she was born, a stand in for you darling. Perhaps the third time it might be his own child. I hope they will be married soon, Julie has finished her course this year, they have been engaged for so long now."

Beth was much happier now that he was 'on the mend' after another week he was allowed to go home. His parents visited and stayed a night with them at the home

Jeremy's parents were Edward and Constance Johnson. His father said Beth could call them by their Christian names or seeing that she had no parents, Mum and Dad. He then went into the bedroom to see Jeremy who was still feeling weak from his illness staying in bed until lunch time.

"You have a lovely place here, Beth; I just cannot understand you doing the work which you choose to do. You are so different to my son's first wife. She was a lovely person a girl after my own heart. She loved dressing up and socialising, she was very popular at parties, always had a full diary. She would have felt buried alive in this place. I can well understand why she did not want a baby, it would have cramped her lifestyle to say nothing of her lovely figure. She knew Jeremy would never agree to an abortion that is why I helped her to have one. One of these days you are going to be taken for a ride by one of these people you encourage maybe robbed."

"Coffee, thank you, Julie. Do help yourself to sugar, Mrs Johnson. Have you taken coffee to the men, Julie?"

"Yes, Beth, they are enjoying Kate's biscuits as well."

"Jeremy will be discussing his future with his father, although he has accepted the GP work for the three villages he also wants to do some other work, either research or specialising in a certain field. We have plenty of room here and can well afford to build a nursing home for his specialist patients; whatever he decides to do I will go along with it. Very soon I am going to appoint an administrator so that I shall be free from the overseeing of the Home. We have departmental managers now who are responsible to me but an administrator would be responsible to the committee as well ... So many have been blessed by coming here and had so much happiness fun and fresh air to say nothing of good wholesome food and gone back happier than they came. I hope you will pardon me for saying so, but I think the first wife must have had a very empty selfish life." Beth could not help saying this.

"Oh she does not think so, I would much prefer Jeremy to have that kind of life to the one he is going to have here, however he and I have never been close friends, he has always been drawn to his father. I do not take kindly to this religious stuff, where has it got you?"

"It has given me peace of mind, God has forgiven me any wrong things I have done and when I die I shall go to Heaven, to the place He has gone to prepare. None of us know what the future holds and what we are going to need. Christianity is no insurance against sickness and loss." Said Bert.

"All right I said I did not want a sermon," she was very put out.

"Come on then, let's go down and have lunch or would you rather have it up here? We usually have meals all together, there often is some lively conversation with the children, not always out of 'the top drawer' but interesting none-the-less,"

"I shall try and put up with it, at least it will not be religious!" said

Beth felt exhausted after dinner. When her husband came up to her sitting room she was very quiet not wanting to tell him what she thought of his mother. However he opened the subject by saying he was sorry he had let her in for an hour with her and not to take any notice what an embittered woman had to say. He knew her so well she would not miss this opportunity to have a 'go' at her.

"Well why did you leave us so long together if you knew?" she was really upset. She also knew he was not strong enough to have a disagreement at this time, his health came first and there would be other times no doubt when she could share her feelings, nevertheless she was awake for a long time feeling very rejected by his mother, not many people had made her feel this way before. "Practice what you preach," she told herself and forgive! It was going to be hard.

Jeremy was in the hospital for a check-up when coming round the corridor he literally bumped into Old Nick. They were so delighted to meet again they had lunch together and Jeremy told him Beth wanted him to meet Roger who was drowned's wife and sons, seeing that he spent the last night with him. He was willing to do that and they fixed a date for a weekend in four weeks' time. In secret he longed to see Beth again, he admired her so much.

The nights were getting darker and once again it was Harvest thanksgiving time. This year the meal was in the church Hall although the food was being prepared at the Home. As usual there was to be a Barn Dance on the Saturday night. It was the weekend Old Nick and Rogers's family were going to be there, Beth was quite happy about that.

Nick arrived on the Friday night, the others on Saturday. Three very angry people presented themselves before lunch and went into the quiet room to chat.

The wife began by saying what a disappointment her husband was to her and how she had to make a life for herself because he would never go out with her to her friends' parties and other social activities.

The boys then became very vocal and angry. "You were never there for us, Mom, don't go blaming it all on to Dad, when we came home from school you would have your friends in for afternoon tea and we would be banished upstairs to our rooms to do homework. When Dad came in he had to do the same and very often you had no dinner for us, you did not care about your family. I knew Dad was stressed out at school but did you ever sit and talk to him and try to understand? No as far as he was concerned he was an under achiever I have heard you shout that at him many times. He obviously felt inferior to your smart friends."

"OK said Nick, I get the picture, it coincides with what he told me during his last night on earth, although I had no idea that's what is was to be. He did say in the eyes of the three of you he was a total failure and the children just did not want to learn what he was teaching them so he was better out of the way. He was going anyway having an inoperable cancer; I think he chose his own time rather than suffer whilst he was tramping round the countryside. Beth dearly wanted him to go into the house and be cared for, she is a nurse but he wanted to stay in the den the boys had made with blankets, so I had a sleeping bag and stayed with him. He talked most of the night and towards day break I said if Beth had been here she would have prayed with him, I could not do that being an unbeliever so we held hands and recited the Lord's Prayer together. Strangely we both felt so peaceful after that and both went to sleep. I left him asleep whilst I went to the house to get some breakfast for us and hot tea. When I returned he was missing. I think while he was so peaceful he felt it was time to go. He forgave you all the things you had done to him as we said, 'forgive us our sins as we forgive those that have sinned against us'. I will tell you I have never felt the same since that night. I envy Beth's faith; she is a wonderful woman and feels called by God to do this work." Nick felt strangely moved by recalling this to Roger's family.

Three people were in tears, when Nick took out his handkerchief there were four. They sat in silence for 15 minutes. When Beth came through the wood to find them, Nick asked her to pray for them to be able to forgive him for the hurt they had felt at his disappearance from their lives and for strength and forgiveness for the future, which she did very lovingly. She then hugged them each in turn, Nick enjoyed his hug saying to himself it was worth coming for that!!

Beth persuaded them after tea to stay the night and go to the Barn Dance with them. After the time in the woods they had to pick up the pieces of life and go on, closure with the past now the father was at peace.

The evening was a huge success the boys entered into it, always short of men at these do's they never had a minute's peace! The Mother was more subdued but quietly chatted to several people.

Sunday afternoon saw the beginning of the Alpha course to be run at Alpha House. Jeremy was in charge of it, seeing that they had it announced in church; about fifteen people turned up. It took the same form as in Africa beginning "Who Jesus is." To Beth`s astonishment Old Nick and Roger's family stayed. Although this was only the first session of ten the churches round the country also were running them so they only had to look on church notice boards to find another one. Beth was shedding tears of gratitude to God for bringing these people to repentance and forgiveness.

Before Rogers's wife went home she asked Beth to pray for her to receive Jesus and the Holy Spirit into her heart and life. Afterwards the radiant smile she gave Beth and the hug said without a doubt it had happened. Nick came every Sunday afternoon for ten weeks to the Alpha course he could not keep away.

Chapter 13

Later that week when the weather was colder and the days darker an 'old banger' of a car pulled up outside the house. A bearded man got out knocked at the door and said he had been told in the village they would let him lodge here for a few weeks. Beth said, "It is the worst time of the year what will you find to do?"

"I am an art teacher wanting to get out of the rat race for a while, I have taken a year off to paint and do what I want to do for a change, I would like to paint the woodlands in winter and this is a perfect place."

With that she invited him in and told him what they did there, the terms and what would he require. When he had seen round the Home he was very impressed some of the boys had asked him about his paintings and why he had such a long beard.

"It is ready for a trim and I will get that done, I am not as old as I look you know, and I hate school as much as you do, I am a teacher!"

"Gosh I never heard of a teacher hating school," Pete said. "I thought they all loved hating the pupils." They seemed to get off to a good start by him promising to give them a lesson if they wanted him to. There was a room at the top of the house where another painter had stayed for a short time with a skylight and bedroom next door. This he welcomed, soon unpacked with the boys' help he made himself at home. Thomas Mann was his name. Over dinner that evening the subject of what he was going to paint in the woods came up again. "I see beauty in everything," he said." Although there are no leaves on the trees there is something to see, who wants to come to the woods tomorrow with me?

Three lads put up their hands and duly presented themselves at breakfast with anoraks woolly scarves and gloves. After they had eaten they went up the woodland path until they found a fallen tree by the river side. They sat together

"Now, boys, sit very quietly, don't even speak if you see something point a finger so that we can all see." They had not long to wait; a rabbit came hopping out of the bracken into a burrow by the river bank. The next thing was a frog swimming down the river near to the side, he then jumped out and burrowed into the bracken to find insects, they actually watched while he found several and ate them quickly. Overhead two squirrels chased each other up the tree trunk jumping from branch to branch having a lovely time. Then more rabbits came scurrying past their little white tails bobbing along. Several moorhens came swimming by dipping their heads into the river looking for food

It was difficult for the boys to sit more than 15 minutes quietly; they had a discussion then about what they had seen," said Thomas. "So often we don't really look for the hidden things under the leaves and in the water."

After their walk they went back into the room Tom had as a studio, each one trying to draw what they seen. This was a good exercise for the boys something quite different from their normal occupation in London.

The days turned into weeks and the weeks years. Julie had finished her course at the collage having a good degree in Hotel management and Nutritional Studies. She and Peter had been engaged for three years whilst she was in college, with Beth looking after Jamie along with Elizabeth. They were like brother and sister, always together. Beth took them to the village play group three mornings a week often taking the children for a walk as she went. Peter treated Jamie as if he was his father as he expected to be one day, however Julie seemed to be reluctant to name the day of her wedding. There was a scheme in college asking for students to go abroad to work in third world countries giving nutritional advice and helping to set up schools for older girls to learn to teach in the existing schools.

After supper one night she asked if she could speak to Beth privately. She outlined what she would like to do asking Beth's advice. "Do you think I am being very selfish wanting to go abroad for six months Beth?" she asked.

"Have you thought this through, Julie? There is Peter to think of and Jamie, how would you fund living for six months in another country, what organisation would you be going with?" Beth was rather concerned.

"You are more like Jamie's mother than I am I could leave him here, in fact if you wanted to you could adopt him and he would be a brother to Elizabeth, they are inseparable at the moment. I am not sure about Peter I do love him but feel I am young and have done nothing yet that is exciting .Oh I am so glad I have been here; where would I have been without you I just dare not think, and if you advise me to forget about this project then I will." Julie was quite emotional.

"Peter regards himself as Jamie's father now he would not want us to adopt him I am sure. Would you still marry Peter when you return?"

"I certainly hope so but I don't know if my feelings will change after I have been away. I certainly don't want to hurt him, he has been wonderful to me. I hardly know how to ask him if I should go. The organisation would pay for my air fare and food whilst I am there, there may be a place there for him to do some agricultural teaching if I enquired." She was very apprehensive.

"I guess you had better talk to Peter, then come back to me; we will pray about it and if the Lord wants you to do this He will make a way for it to happen. We shall miss you and if Peter goes we'll miss him even more! But someone else will turn up I am sure. Off you go and find him I will give the children their story now," replied Beth.

Were there going to be changes on the way? Things were going so smoothly in the home no real problems, but Beth would not stand in the way of Julie having a bit of excitement in her life, she was a good girl.

The next morning Jeremy asked Beth if they could spend some time together. "You are always so busy, Beth, we never get the chance to talk these days. I have an afternoon free, shall we go out for tea and leave the children here with Julie?"

They walked up through the woods to their favourite picnic spot by the river. Not picnic weather but they were warm in anoraks. "Now what do you want to say to me. Have I done something to upset you? I have felt a coolness in our relationship recently, Jeremy, come on and tell me."

"I do not feel a person in my own right, Beth. I am known as 'Beth's husband'. You are the king pin in this establishment I am an accessory and I want to be more and do more in my life." Oh dear, Beth thought, not another one after Julie!

"My darling, people think that of me perhaps because I have been the 'king pin' as you put it, before you came and when you were abroad. I include you in all the discussions I make how else can I include you unless you want a specific job like an administrator or something?" Beth did not like this conversation wondering what was in his mind." You are the GP for three villages and have surgeries in each one how else could you take more work on?"

"I could set up a health centre in our village or even on our land here, not only a surgery but rooms for Health Visitors, Community Nurses, Dentistry, Minor operations which would stop the long journey to Swansea, Probably take another doctor in with me to share the work and calls at night. We would need an administrator and two midwives to make it a real going concern. Instead of being under Swansea they would all be contained here where it would be so much more hands on."

"That sounds absolutely wonderful, Jamie, you obviously have given it a lot of thought. I am with you all the way. How can you make this happen?"

"I have made preliminary enquiries and am hoping to meet the NHS planning committee in the next week to sound them out. I think my initial letter was well received and set them thinking. It will mean more work but more interesting doing minor ops, in time we might buy them an X-ray machine so that people would not have make a long journey to Swansea."

He sounded so enthusiastic, Beth was delighted. She then told him about Julie wanting to go abroad and possibly Peter, He thought it would be a good thing for them to do, it would be no problem looking after Jamie but he wondered about adoption, he was willing but what would happen when they came back.

The next day Beth gave Jeremy the architect's phone number, Zachary in Swansea, to invite him round to discuss the needs of a Health Centre and make plans. One of the fields Beth had retained for the home backed on to the village, she would be quite happy for that to be used for bringing the cost down. If that funded the building then the NHS could pay them the rent. Beth called a committee meeting for the next week, Jeremy put forward his plan for the three villages enthusiastically, which was met with 'all in favour', with the promise of the plans and architect at the next meeting in two weeks' time.

Later that night Beth took a walk by the river and suddenly felt depressed. Changes were things she did not like especially when she was not making them. She wondered if she was jealous of Jamie's sudden longing for this Health Centre with a similar enthusiasm to her own when setting up the Alpha Home. She sat in the summer house and thought what have I achieved? Was her mother-in-law right when she had criticized her use of the money left by her parents? "Lord show me what to think, I have done this for your glory, but do not see many fruits spiritually for my labours. I know you wanted me to do this, please confirm that it is right to carry on and please bless Jeremy and guide him to make the right discussions for this new venture."

As she sat there into her mind came the account in the old Testament of Elijah after God had honoured him whilst the prophets of Baal called upon their false Gods to burn the sacrifice on the alter which of course they did not. When Elijah prayed to the Living God fire came and consumed his sacrifice proving to the prophets of Baal that He was the all-powerful one and He answered Elijah's prayer. Then we see in the next chapter he was afraid of Jezebel who was out to kill him. Even after God's victory Satan came to him to cause him to doubt and be afraid of the enemy. But God had not forgotten him and sent a woman to give him some food to physically strengthen him then his faith was restored. Beth thanked the Lord for the remainder of his greatness, that her work would be rewarded in Heaven. She felt renewed as she went back into supper! Yes she was hungry. That night the story was about Elijah and how God used him greatly in spite of him and us having Satan to try and get us away from trusting and serving Him.

Chapter 14

Two weeks after this experience Beth was in the orchard picking some apples when a smart young man came purposefully through the trees.

"Hello, Miss Beth, remember me, Jacko?"

"Well I would not have recognised you, Jacko, you look very smart so happy and relaxed. Have you walked from the village?"

"Yes and really enjoyed being around here again. Many times I would like to have written to you but somehow never got round to doing it so I thought at the first opportunity I would come and see you to tell you in person my story."

"I will go and get some food you must be hungry would you like it out here or inside? Also are you staying with us tonight?" Beth was so pleased to see him; he was so different to how she remembered him, the ring leader!

"Yes if I can stay I would like to and eating out here would be super, thank you very much, Miss Beth, it is like old times it has not altered. I'm so glad."

In a short time Beth made sandwiches put fruit and cake a pot of tea and mugs and plates on the tray. Jamie and Elizabeth came from the field to join them for a sandwich.

They were only babies when he was at the home how quickly the years had gone by almost five.

After eating Beth said, "I cannot wait to hear what you are going to tell me, Jacko, so eat up quickly I am all ears," she thought it must be good.

"You knew that I was the leader of our gang in London. We often met and fought with rival gangs in different streets. Very often wounding some members of the gang, the more the merrier we thought. We were known to the police especially me as the gang leader; we lied to get out of trouble so they never believed a word we said. When I went home from here you may not believe it but I remembered a lot of your stories, and I felt different going back to the gang. What we were doing was not right and I told them so. They thought I had gone 'soft' so they replaced me which made me look silly but I was pleased. I still went around with them until one day one of the teachers had threatened one of the lads so the gang was called together to see what to do with her. They planned to get her after school, she stayed late for some reason on Tuesdays so it was planned next Tuesday they would be in the car park when everyone had gone home but her. I would not go with them so they beat me up but I still would not go. I stood round the back of the school out of sight and waited I should have warned her really, but out she came and they set on to her. I heard her scream, one of them had a knife and slashed her arm and leg the others kicked her. They then ran off and I ran to her to see what I could do to help. She was bleeding badly and I called an ambulance, I tied my school tie round her arm to stop the bleeding and her stocking round her leg then the police came, she did see me briefly before going unconscious. Of course with my record the police carted me off to the police station they would not believe me when I told them I was helping her and not with the gang. But it was no use.

"To cut a long story short we went to court and were sent to different detention centres. No one would believe me when I told them about you and knowing it was wrong. But going to the detention was the best thing that happened to me, God's way of sorting me out. Even my dad said I was no good now for shoplifting and he beat me up as well.

"I asked if I could do some school work and the teacher at the detention centre took a liking to me and gave me lots of homework to do in the evenings. I did not mix with a lot of the boys there because they were no better than I had been. There was a chaplain there who I talked to but before I met him I found a book in the drawer and started to read it, to my surprise I read about some of the stories you used to tell us at night in bed. The chaplain helped me to understand what I was reading and how to pray. I became a Christian and one Sunday in Church in the centre I stood up and told them about you and the Home and how I had now become a Christian."

"Two years after I had been there I had a visitor and it was the school teacher. She had been very ill after the attack and nearly lost her life but she remembered me binding up her arm with my tie. Of course she knew me and asked the police what happened to me. She told them the truth and asked if she could visit me. I told her that coming here was the best thing that could have happened to me, I was now studying for O levels, had become a Christian and every Sunday was helping the chaplain set up the church and learning to play the piano. She said she was so pleased that I was not angry and hurt that she did not do more to get me out. I do not want to go out, I am staying as long as possible. Now Miss Beth I have 6 O levels and thank God that he worked it all out for good as the Bible says."

Beth was crying when he had finished God had not sent a widow woman with food as for Elijah but a boy with a changed life who could have been a crook for the rest of his life. "Come, Jacko, let us thank the Lord." And under the apple tree she poured out her heart in thanksgiving to God. The Home had served its purpose, if only for one lad and she felt very uplifted; she hugged him and said he could stay as long as he liked and even work there until he knew what the next thing was he wanted to do.

Jeremy as going to need another doctor, as they discussed this Beth said, "Who better than Old Nick?"

"Excellent," said Jeremy. "He is working in London but hates the hospital life. I have got his address and phone number; shall I ring and ask him to come down for the weekend when he is free?

"Yes, please do, he is a good friend to us both and in sympathy with the work here. I will never forget him sleeping with the chap who we found in the river the next morning, it made a profound impression on him, also he saw the wife and two sons afterwards. It would be good having him here, even better if he had a wife, he might have now but I think we would have had an invite to the wedding if he was married." Beth was enthusiastic.

Old Nick came down three weeks later and brought an old friend from nurse training days who Beth was very fond of. "Well, Nick, this is a real bonus bringing Sally Anne with you I am delighted."

"She is the nearest I could find to you, she is very special and very much like you in her ways and beliefs; we go to church every Sunday and I am nearly 'there'," he said with a twinkle in his eye. "Come on then, old chap, let's hear all about this new venture whist the girls go and make up for lost time."

They certainly did that; it was a bonus having Sally Anne for the weekend. Beth told her all about the Home, some stories about things that had happened there and wondering what the future held. "If the Health Centre takes off, Sally Anne, would you like to come and work here, that's of course if Nick comes in with Jeremy? It is very different to a London setting here, so quiet, but a lot going on to get involved in."

"I think I would be very happy down here, nursing is very different now to when we trained, Beth, so much paperwork which takes up the time we should be with the patients. I had considered going into the community to be nearer the patients, but to be working hands-on in this new venture would be super."

"I have not dared to mention it but a Nursing Home would be a great help as well. We have enough land to spare and if the finances continue to even out with the cost of the Home I am sure it would be an asset," said Beth.

The weekend went all too quickly; Nick said he would think about the situation and let Jeremy know his decision in the near future.

In the meantime Julie was getting excited about her coming adventure. Jeremy decided that Beth should have a holiday before she went so that Julie could look after the children whilst she was away. He could not go with her at this critical time with plans and interviews with the Health Authority. It was all going very well, he could manage without Beth for a week.

As usual Beth prayed about it and as she prayed a picture of a vineyard came into her mind, "That is it; I will go to Spain and see a few of the vines I have invested in." So having made up her mind and after talking to Jeremy, she rang Jake to see if he wanted her to go.

"You are most welcome, Beth, we have a very large house and a lovely lady who is a widow looking after us, she has two children ten and twelve years old who also live here. My friend and business partner and I get on so well working together, we welcome you who made all this possible. When can you come?" He sounded like the old Jake, happy and relaxed.

"Is next week too soon for you?" she asked.

"No, come to Alicante and Maria will meet you there, we are very busy at the moment otherwise I would come. Let me know when to expect you. Look forward to seeing you, 'bye now!"

Suddenly Beth wanted to get away. Other than an occasional trip to London and Cardiff she had not had a holiday for five years. When she came back they would have a party celebrating the first five years. Things were going smoothly at the Home, everyone was doing his or her job very well and did not need her supervision. Jacko was working with Peter in the market garden along with the others, Tom the painter spent a lot of time with the children, he loved swimming and gave them lessons in the pool.

Jeremy took Beth to Cardiff airport to see her off. He was not at all sure this was a good thing, but he was too enthusiastic in the new venture to go anywhere with her. He gave her a hug and a kiss then she was off to the departure gate feeling light-hearted, leaving her cares behind.

The flight was on time after Beth had passed through customs she went towards the entrance of the airport to find Maria standing with her name on a placard. Happily she joined her, soon to be speeding to the vineyard. She was a little apprehensive of her reception. She had not met Simon, Jake's partner. Maria talked a lot about the house and way of life that seemed to suit them all. She was a widow with a boy of 12 years and a girl of 10, who loved the life at school and working with Jake and Simon when they were very busy with the vines. They earned their pocket money willingly.

They arrived home in time for lunch which was soup and salad with homemade crusty bread and cheese. Jake and Simon came in around two o'clock. Beth need not have been apprehensive all was very jolly. Jake was anxious to give Beth all the details of the house which came with the furniture when they bought the vineyard. There were six bedrooms – he stressed they all had their own rooms – one large sitting room and a family room where they often sat after dinner to watch television. Two smaller sitting rooms,   one where Maria did her sewing and the children did their homework; the other where the men had their office; where they often spent long hours working out the books and finances.

The basement housed the washing machine and a games room housing a billiard table and all the things no one could find a home for. The household furniture was beautiful. The previous owners must have been very wealthy. Apparently one day they felt they had had enough, getting older they wanted to be near a distant relative and called Simon in to tell him. He had worked for them faithfully for 15 years, they had treated him like their own son. They lowered the price to rock bottom hoping that he would be able to buy it. They were overjoyed when he found Jake who came up with the deposit. Jake told all this to Beth on their walk round the fields after dinner.

Dinner was a happy meal. Maria's children were there – Roberta known as Robbie and Alfonso known as Fonso. They were not shy, asking many questions about England. Beth invited them to Wales as soon as they would like to come. She then told them of the work she did at the home.

Sitting under the trellis where bougainvillaea of several colours cascaded around them was idyllic. Maria was a very good cook and had made a tasty Spanish dish with peaches and cream to follow.

"I can tell you are here in paradise, Jake," she said after dinner. "I do not blame you for not wanting to live in England again."

"Beth that last winter almost finished me off, all the snow and being cut off even from the village was my undoing. I was so sorry to let you down but it was my only cowardly way and I am sorry."

"Don't you worry about that, I knew what God wanted me to do, but I knew you would not want to do it buying the old Manor house, and so going was the right thing for you to do. Remember all things work together for the good to those who love God and are called according to His purpose."

At the mention of God Maria's smile disappeared and she looked very sad. She had suffered losing her husband and needed comfort After the men had gone into their room to do office work, Maria sent the children to bed, she then spoke of her distress at losing her husband in an accident and of how she blamed God for taking him away from them. Beth then told her about her own loss of her parents and then Jake, she talked about the free will that God had given to us all to use as we wanted to. "If we choose to love and serve Him He makes provision for us it may not be as we would want, I wanted Jake and I to be together although I knew it would not be a proper marriage. He did love me but not as a wife and he wanted me to meet the right man to experience married love, and I have done, but if I had had my way and he had stayed I would never have known that or started the Alpha Home."

Maria thought for some time then said, "I see now that God had made provision for me here. There will never be another husband for me but we are a family here, in a way I have two husbands! They care for me and my children and we feel secure."

"Then let us thank God for His provision for you in finding you a new home and a family to care for." With that Beth prayed with Maria and they both felt better, a close relationship later formed to last many years.

The next day Beth enjoyed wandering round the fields of vines, the grapes had formed but not matured. All hands were needed to tie up the vines to the frames and wires keeping them off the ground. The children were working on that, too, so Beth asked them to show her how and she also helped. The beautiful sunshine caused her to fetch her sun lotion which resulted in a super tan! After dinner that night she was so tired physically but asked Jake if it would be possible for her to go to Guadalest to see the road where her parents coach left the road.

"Do you really want to go? It will cause you some pain, Beth. There is a plaque to say what happened at the spot several people lost their lives there many were injured and the driver killed. I will take you if you really want to go"

On Sunday no outside work was done, a day of rest. The chaps did the cooking usually but this week Simon and Jake took Beth up the mountain road and had lunch at the Monastery on top of the mountain. It was painful for Beth as she stood viewing the place where the coach went down. Simon put his arms round her and wept with her. He was a loving fellow, he understood far more than Jake what her feelings were. She knew her parents were in heaven and that was a real comfort to her

The day before Beth went home they had a party for her. She and Maria made the food during the day, in the evening about twenty friends and neighbours tuned up with lots of small gifts of food. The record player worked overtime. After the meal out on the patio the dancing began, a bit like the barn dances at home with lots of laughing, back-slapping and gaiety. The general feeling was why did Bethany come all this way to see her ex-husband when she had another at home? She told them she wanted to know how they made the wine.

Beth would like to have stayed longer, she felt so relaxed in this strange household; she loved the children there, to say nothing of the super weather, so it was with great reluctance she was driven by Jake to the airport the next evening.

"Are you happy with what you have seen, Beth?"

"Oh yes I am. I love Simon, Maria and the children; the whole set up is wonderful. You work very hard all of you and have created a real family there. I would love to return one day with Jeremy and our children when you need extra help, we could do something like picking the grapes for you, would you mind us coming, you are so much better here in the sunshine. We're back to what we were in the crypt in London, our old friendship restored." Beth was delighted with the outcome of their relationship.

"We would welcome you and anyone else you would like to bring. Cheerio, Beth, God bless you, you have done us all good being here, especially Maria."

"Thank you, Lord," she said as the plane took off for home "it truly has been a wonderful experience."

Beth found it hard coming down to earth after her week in Spain. Julie told her of their wedding plans. Peter wanted to get married before she left to help the third world youngsters. There was a possibility of a place for Peter in an agricultural collage teaching about crops etc., which would be better if they were married. The date was to be the 1st of August when five years of the home was to be celebrated.

"You are sure you want to marry Peter, Julie, you have been engaged a long time, I know you love him but why have you waited all this time?"

"I wanted to wait until I was fully qualified before getting married, I am only twenty two now and Jamie will be five then," she said.

Jeremy made a big fuss of Beth on her return, he had missed her. No one to talk to when he came home in the evenings, although they spoke on the phone. He missed her in bed as well! The plans for the Health Centre were ready to go into the council offices he and Zachary had become good friends over the past three months. When the news leaked out the villagers were so delighted to hear it, they stopped Jeremy in the street to ask the latest news! Meanwhile he went to many health centres to get ideas. He *was* still waiting for Old Nick's final answer on re-joining him.

"We have visitors, Beth, a Mr Bryce Jones and his sister would like to see you," said Rachel on the phone extension in the greenhouse. After tying the vines she wanted more of a hands-on existence, she had the boys, Jamie and Elizabeth filling pots with compost ready for her to put in plug plants for summer flowering. She hastily left them in Peter's care and went to get changed to meet her old friends the previous owners.

With a little hesitation she walked into her sitting room. Jonathon the first on his feet with arms outstretched to welcome her gave her a bear hug! Chloe his sister was more reserved. "I cannot believe the quiet little princess you were to me is the mistress of our old home!"

"Quiet little mouse is more my description than princess. How are you both? Looking very well and prosperous. It must seem strange coming back to your old home and finding a going concern," said Beth.

"We are quite speechless," he said, "do tell us how it all happened, are these all your children beside the river fishing?"

"No they are children from London who come down for two weeks holiday to get acquainted with the countryside animals, to find out where milk really comes from, and some don't like it, we have to put it in containers at first to get them used to it. We also have paying guests, an artist who seems to have taken up residence here and sometimes teenagers who need time to sort themselves out. I sold the farm to fund this place but now we are self-funding, selling eggs and garden produce in Swansea market and also the village shops. After you have finished your tea we can walk around if you are not too tired."

They spent the next hour walking around looking at the new buildings, the swimming pool, and the tea shop. When at last they got to the quiet place Beth explained it was a place of meditation, used for talks and concerts.

Chloe then spoke quite firmly, "I am not into this God stuff and I don't know how you can be when your parents were killed, he did that to you. I have had two husbands, two divorces and no children, is that what a supposedly loving God does?"

"God gives us all a free will; the driver of the coach used his to drink alcohol before driving, killing people and injuring others, you cannot blame God for that. I, too, have been divorced, Jake happened to like men better than women and so left me to go round the world. Incidentally I have just spent a week with him and his household in Spain where I invested in a vineyard, he and his friend work growing grapes and making wine. I made a mistake, not God. But He has brought good out of the situation and I now have a loving husband who is the local GP and try to bring happiness to many others who would not know the peacefulness of the countryside. Sorry to be doing all the talking. How are your parents?"

"Dad died of a heart attack Ten years ago. Mother is still alive with terminal cancer, she has had chemotherapy and an operation. She is in a nursing home near Bristol, we have just been to see her and thought we would like to see our old home again. Mother is very difficult nothing satisfies her but then she always has been. This place must have been in a terrible mess, Beth, having been empty for so long but we love it now, it is better than it ever was in our younger days," said Johnathon. And with that he gave her another big hug.

"Now it is almost dinner time and Jeremy will soon be at home from the surgery. He has done five years research in Africa for the AIDS foundation. Would you like to stay for the night? We have guest rooms always made up we never know who might come along."

"That would be good we would have to have found a hotel for the night. I live in Scotland and am driving back tomorrow. Chloe is nearer Bristol so that she can visit Mother. I have a wife and two children at home; we live in a very old house with lots of gardens around and I work as the manager of a factory making tartan cloth." He gave a picture of a settled happy family life.

Jeremy came in just before dinner time and was introduced Jonathan was pleased to meet him but it was obvious Cloe did not care for the opposite sex! They all had dinner together with the staff and children. As usual the children kept up the conversation telling them what they got up to in London, the more they could shock the listeners the more the children liked it. Quite a hilarious meal

"Did you really live here when you were young" they asked. "You must have been like the queen in the palace living here."

. It was not like it is today, Geoff. It was cold in the winter, the kitchen was the warmest place the bedrooms cold and the wind whistled down the chimneys; it always seemed to rain a lot. I was glad when they sent me to boarding school, although I missed Miss Beth. We were not royal but rather poor in some ways. The summers were the best time when we camped out in the woods and tree house which we made ourselves, then we went up the hill to Beth's farm to ride her horse. We were sent to boarding school out of Mother's way which Chloe hated but to me this area was wonderful to come back to."

"I hate school and will do anything to miss games and maths." The others agreed. "It must be awful living in a school you could not get away from, did you ever run away?" said Geoff.

"Not really I would only have been brought back and punished, I thought it was better to work hard and get good results from my exams and a better job after leaving school." Dinner was over now and it was time for bed.

"Time to tell a story to the children, Johnathon, Jeremy will be in our sitting room now and then I will join you for coffee," said Beth.

"I would like to hear the story if I may, Chloe can keep Jeremy company until we get back." And so it was that he sat on one of the beds whilst it began.

"The story tonight is about two people who had been at the crucifixion of Jesus and I think were part of His followers. They were disappointed and saddened because they had seen him doing many miraculous things, healing the sick and even raising one man who had died, they did not expect Jesus to die like a criminal. They were going home miserably sad when suddenly someone came up the road and started talking to them. They were surprised when he asked them why they were sad; they thought everyone in Jerusalem knew what had happened. They started telling Him then they reached their home and invited Jesus in to have supper with them. He started telling them all about the Old Testament stories, he knew such a lot of things, and I guessed that they knew He was a special person. Then when the bread came out he reached out and took it, broke it up and as he gave it to them they saw the wounds in his hands where He had been nailed to the cross. Suddenly they knew who he was and He vanished from them, they were so delighted they put their coats on and rushed back to Jerusalem to tell His other followers that Jesus was alive they had seen and talked to Him. That was not the only time he saw them before He went back to heaven to be with His Father, God. Have you ever been sad not understanding what was going on, miserable? I have and when that happens I remember this story that really happened, and sometimes Jesus sends somebody to talk to me and help, other times I pray and ask God to help me and show me what to do. Jesus died on the cross to forgive us for the wrong things we all have done like some of the things you were talking about at dinner time ... then He helps us not to do those things again. If you want to know more or I can be of any help I shall be in the quiet place tomorrow after breakfast. Good night, boys, and God bless you all." With that she kissed them all and turned off the light.

In the corridor Johnathan said, "Don't I get a kiss for listening? Beth, you are a good story teller I almost believed you."

"How can you say that, every word was true I have experienced all that I spoke about. Jesus is very real to me. That is the reason I have given my inheritance to Him and do this work. I have seen a few lives changed. We do not preach at them just tell a story from the Bible when they are in bed and love them. They often come to the quiet place and ask for more. Why is Chloe so withdrawn, she has hardly spoken since she came"?

"Too many memories I think. Our Mother was always at odds with my Father over things mostly money. She insisted that we went to boarding school to get rid of us and that affected Chloe more than me, she was very unhappy. Unfortunately she took that unhappiness into two marriages both nice chaps who deserved better. In some ways she is like our Mother discontented and enjoys being miserable. Mother has no pain she sleeps well eats well is able to look after herself far more than the others in the home and yet is miserable, I am always glad when the visit is over," he replied.

Jeremy and Chloe were drinking coffee and seemed to be getting along very well. They all talked about the things they used to get up to as children around the place, Jeremy was envious.

"Do the nights get shorter Beth as one gets older?" with one eye open Jeremy was reluctant to get out of bed. Beth threw a pillow at him "Come on and say good bye to Chloe she fancies you I can tell."

He jumped out of bed and ran to her and gave her a bear hug, "My darling you are the only one for me I could have had millions of offers in past years queuing up for my attention but I only wanted you," kissing her soundly they both dissolved into fits of laughter "I hear the patter of little feet they are ready for breakfast and so am I come on!" They joined Johnathan and Chloe for breakfast, the boys were not up yet and the workers had all gone about their work.

After a walk in the woods for old time's sake they went on their way, promising to come back another day. Jeremy had talked about the new Health Centre, Chloe rather fancied him and thought she might get a job there if they needed a secretary, she could live in the village. She was always jealous of Beth as a child and if she could get even by taking her husband from her she would be satisfied.

"Will you come to Zachary's office with me this morning, Beth, I want to finalise the plans, I need your help with the decor seating, etc."

"My advice will cost you a lunch at the King John Inn," she said.

"What a good idea all on our own we could look out some chairs for the surgery, not too comfortable, we don't want them to sit there too long! While we are there you could get your wedding outfit for Julie's wedding in four weeks' time.

After lunch they went shopping, the first shop they went in she found a gold coloured suit with navy blue accessories which suited her very well Jeremy sat and watched "Do you remember what you wore on our wedding day? You could wear that and be a sensation."

"What, a swim suit and see-through flowered wrap around? That was wonderful for me I did not even know I was going to be married until three days before!" she remembered lovingly.

They enjoyed their trip into town picking up the children from the nursery on the way home. Beth spoke to Julie about the wedding preparations that evening. Now that she had departmental managers and an administrator. She had more free time to do the things with the children again. Some of them enjoyed talking to the animals, she found one boy telling Daisy the cow all about visiting his father in prison. There were still a few small lambs in a small pen, one boy spent a lot of time just sitting in the pen stroking one lamb that had taken a fancy to him. They were quite tame having been fed with a feeding bottle. This was all therapeutic and Beth often saw a real change not only in behaviour but social skills in talking to each other without name-calling and swearing. Even the hens came running towards them more for what they were going to get than friendship, but the children though it was them they loved, they enjoyed feeding the animals and ducks on the river bank.

The wedding day was fast approaching, Jamie and Elizabeth were to be attendants both dressed in cream, a shirt trousers and bow tie for Jamie, and a full skirted long dress for Elizabeth with white shoes and gloves. Mary was to be bridesmaid in a long lavender dress carrying a bunch of roses of various colours out of the garden. Elizabeth to carry a basket of sweet peas and Jamie a small cushion with the two rings pinned on it. Coming out of the quiet room after the wedding the children were going to scatter rose petals from the garden along the carpet where Julie walked with Peter. Julie's father was to give her away and James, his brother, was to be the best man.

The house was filled with flowers, the gardens had never looked better. The Staff past and present had all had invitations designed by Tom who was still in the attic painting, Old Nick was coming bringing Sally Ann with him.

Julie's parents were staying at the home for several nights. The outside caterers were booked and Beth thought everything was in place. Jacko was so proud to be the door keeper giving out the wedding order of service leaflets, in a new suit! After the wedding a short thanksgiving time was to be conducted by Father Joseph who was also doing the wedding.

An hour before the wedding Beth went in to help Julie get dressed. Jeremy and Nick were preparing Peter and dressing him with much hilarity. Beth went into Julie and together they prayed and thanked the Lord for the past five years and asked for His presence at the ceremony today. Then she lifted the dress over her head which fell in long swathes to the ground. The hairdresser had drawn Julie's golden hair into a pretty French plear, so Beth placed the veil and tiara on her head which sparkled in the sun light, she looked beautiful. They had difficulty in Peter and Julie keeping apart all morning.

All set now, time to go. The quiet place was packed with friends and villagers. Julie and Peter's relatives were present, Kate and Bill proudly supporting Peter their nephew. The wedding march was played on the electric organ by the church organist as Julie on her father's arm came down the aisle to meet Peter. The children preceded her and Mary behind. The wedding service was solemn but joyful hymns sang lustily. The vows sincerely made and a message by Father Joseph. After the marriage ceremony they all sat down and Joseph began to talk of the last five years of the home."

"I have not got the time to tell you of all the work that has gone on here these past five years. We have been bringing children down from London more or less every two months for holidays and many of them have joined our church and even sing in the choir as a result. They are not preached at, just given a short Bible story when they go to bed, but many lives have been changed as a result," Jacko called out from the back of the room, "Mine certainly has," to everyone's amusement!

Then Julie got up and turned to the congregation

"It is not usual for the bride to speak at her wedding but I have to say that I am the first lame duck who Beth took under her wing. I was in London on the streets when Beth gave me soup. I was pregnant and my parents were so disappointed in me they asked me to leave. Beth brought me down here and we moved into this home shortly afterwards. Jamie was born five years ago in July, the first here. We met a very disgruntled doctor, Jeremy, who told Beth to get on with the delivery! (everybody laughed). You see he has changed as a result of the Alpha Home, although everybody who has changed for the better has not had to marry Beth to do so. (more laughter) I just thank the Lord that I have found Him here to be my Saviour, the Alpha course which we run every September taught me a lot about the Christian life. Peter was with me when Jamie was born, and we have been engaged for a long time. He was also holding Beth's hand when Elizabeth came into the world, Jamie was ill in Africa at the time. I am hoping that the next time it will be his child being born not he being a proxy father (more laughter). Thank you Beth and Jeremy for all your love and care. I can never repay you enough. They encouraged me to go to college and get a degree. Soon Peter and I will be leaving to go to a third world country to work in Nutrition and agriculture and spread the good news of Jesus Christ to those there in similar circumstances to us. Jamie is staying here until we see how things are out there. Alpha Home meant a new beginning for me. Thank you for listening to me." Many hankies were evident after she sat down.

Beth then spoke of her last five years wishing her parents could have been there. "What of the next five years? More of the same as well as a new venture for Jeremy in building the new Health Centre in the village. Nick, his friend and known tOo many here, is joining him in partnership, you will all be seeing much more of them although I guess you are hoping not in their official capacity. As for me I am going nowhere." Jeremy jumped up and said, "That is where you are wrong, open this envelope and see where you are going. Beth has worked very hard always thinking of other people how she can try and make their lives better, come on Beth tell us," he said.

"A trip to Florida, Disney World for two weeks with Jamie and Elizabeth. Thank you so much we will love that, being a family together. Thank you all for coming and making this day so special." As she sat down Tom the artist came to the front with a parcel, he had painted a portrait of her to be hung he said inside the porch door of the quiet place. He added his thanks to Julie's and how much The Alpha Home meant to him.

The bridal couple walked down the aisle, the children throwing rose petals before them. Everyone was so happy, the sun was shining, the river sparkling kisses and hugs amongst the guests. Jeremy hugged Julie and said, "Come to that irritable handsome doctor who would not deliver Jamie!" She felt like a daughter to him and Beth.

The food was a banquet, a marquee in the orchard with pink and white frills and swathes of silk material from the roof of the tent, with pink carpet on the floor. The champagne flowed and were speeches made, it was indeed a very happy time. The bride and groom stayed until very late before going to a hotel for the night and flying off the next morning from Cardiff to tour the west coast of America.

Towards midnight Beth and Jeremy wandered out after the children were in bed and walked by the river in the moonlight. They finally rested in the summer house and talked of all the things that had happened in the last five years. They were thankful to God for each other for the dark times in their lives which enabled them to understand the feelings of those who came to seek their help. Also the joy of fulfilment in each other, the expectation of a lovely holiday in America."

"I chose a villa with a maid rather than a hotel, Beth, because we then can be a family for two weeks and I will have your undivided attention! When we come back I will be busy as well as you but need you to help me set things up in the village to bring the healing from the Lord to those who need

Him. We can never stop thanking Him for leading us to do what He did when on earth, heal the body, mind and spirit."

The characters in this story are fictitious, the spiritual experiences which have been written about are very real and have been experienced by the author. The Alpha Course originated at the Holy Trinity Anglican Church at Brompton, London many years ago. It is known and embraced by all denominations of the Christian church worldwide in many languages. If after reading the book you would like to know more about the Alpha Course contact Holy Trinity Church. They would be pleased to help.